Memories Of That Night In Her Room Had Haunted His Dreams For Years

He could see Katie in her nightgown, feel the guilt for not being able to look away. But he still couldn't. After all this time, he would've given his right arm to make love to her right there on her bed.

Now, after all these years, he was going to be sleeping in her house again. The thought of spending the night with her was enough to make him sweat. It had been a while since he'd been with a woman, and he was hungry. Had he been back in New York, there would have been a number of women he could have called, any of whom would have been more than happy to share his bed. But he knew he was kidding himself. Even if he was back in the city, he wouldn't call those women. There was only one woman he wanted to make love to tonight.

And her name was Katie Devonworth.

Dear Reader,

We're so glad you've chosen Silhouette Desire because we have a *lot* of wonderful—and sexy!—stories for you. The month starts to heat up with *The Boss Man's Fortune* by Kathryn Jensen. This fabulous boss/secretary novel is part of our ongoing continuity, DYNASTIES: THE DANFORTHS, and also reintroduces characters from another well-known family: The Fortunes. Things continue to simmer with Peggy Moreland's *The Last Good Man in Texas,* a fabulous continuation of her series THE TANNERS OF TEXAS.

More steamy stuff is heading your way with *Shut Up And Kiss Me* by Sara Orwig, as she starts off a new series, STALLION PASS: TEXAS KNIGHTS. (Watch for the series to continue next month in Silhouette Intimate Moments.) The always-compelling Laura Wright is back with a hot-blooded Native American hero in *Redwolf's Woman. Storm of Seduction* by Cindy Gerard will surely fire up your hormones with an alpha male hero out of your wildest fantasies. And Margaret Allison makes her Silhouette Desire debut with *At Any Price,* a book about sweet revenge that is almost too hot to handle!

And, as summer approaches, we'll have more scorching love stories for you—guaranteed to satisfy your every Silhouette Desire!

Happy reading,

Melissa Jeglinski

Melissa Jeglinski
Senior Editor, Silhouette Desire

Please address questions and book requests to:
Silhouette Reader Service
U.S.: 3010 Walden Ave., P.O. Box 1325, Buffalo, NY 14269
Canadian: P.O. Box 609, Fort Erie, Ont. L2A 5X3

AT ANY PRICE

MARGARET ALLISON

Published by Silhouette Books
America's Publisher of Contemporary Romance

SILHOUETTE BOOKS

ISBN 0-373-76584-3

AT ANY PRICE

Copyright © 2004 by Cheryl Klam

This edition published by arrangement with Harlequin Books S.A.

® and TM are trademarks of Harlequin Books S.A., used under license.
Trademarks indicated with ® are registered in the United States Patent
and Trademark Office, the Canadian Trade Marks Office and in other
countries.

Visit Silhouette Books at www.eHarlequin.com

Printed in U.S.A.

MARGARET ALLISON

was raised in the suburbs of Detroit, Michigan, and received a B.A. in political science from the University of Michigan. A former marketing executive, she has also worked as a model and actress. She is the author of several novels, and *At Any Price* marks her return to the world of romance after taking some time off to care for her young children. Margaret currently divides her time between her computer, the washing machine and the grocery store. She loves to hear from readers. Please write to her c/o Silhouette Books, 233 Broadway, Suite 1001, New York, NY 10279.

For my mom, Barbara Robinson, with thanks and love.

One

Katie sat in the sleek waiting room of Jack Reilly's office. He owned the whole building, a glass high-rise smack in the middle of Manhattan.

She knew Jack was a big deal now; heck, everyone in Newport Falls knew he was a self-made multimillionaire. But seeing it was a different story.

It had taken every ounce of her courage to set foot inside Reilly Investments. She kept reminding herself that this was Jack, her childhood friend, not Donald Trump. She shouldn't be intimidated. After all, she had nursed Jack through colds, chicken pox and fights with his father.

But still, the lump that was lodged in her throat would not go away. And the little voice inside her that kept telling her to run, the one that kept telling her what a mistake it was to come here, would not shut up.

She wondered if she would recognize the man described in the papers as the confident, brash millionaire. Sure, Jack had always been a little cocky, but she knew better. She could see right through the artificial confidence to the insecure boy underneath. He had been painfully aware of where he had come from and who he was. His cockiness was just covering up the insecurity of being the poorest kid in school.

She smoothed her hair, certain she looked a mess. It was only noon, yet her day had begun eight hours earlier. She had taken care of some business at the paper before borrowing Marcella's car for the drive into the city. She felt bad about putting the extra miles on her friend's already worn car, but she had little choice. Not without the funds to repair her broken-down car or afford the train or plane fare. Since her divorce, money was tight. And the newspaper, her family's business for generations, had been hemorrhaging money. She had stopped paying herself a salary months ago.

Katie checked her watch again. Nearly one-thirty. Their lunch appointment had been for twelve forty-five.

Perhaps there had been a mix-up, perhaps Jack didn't even know he was meeting with her today. After all, she had not spoken with him directly. All their communication had been through his assistant. Katie hadn't told Jack's assistant that she wanted to ask the big-time investor for a loan for her failing newspaper. She hadn't told her that Jack Reilly was more than an old friend. Much more.

In fact, she had loved Jack from the moment she first set eyes on him. She had been convinced they were meant for each other, sure that the friendship they had nurtured since kindergarten was destined for passion. But she was wrong. And to this day, she had only admitted her love for Jack to one other person: Jack himself.

She blushed as she remembered that day, fourteen years before. In senior year of high school she and Jack had been part of a group of three friends. Jack Reilly, Matt O'Malley and Katie Devonworth. Inseparable in school and out, they were known throughout Newport Falls as earth, wind and fire. Katie, the daughter of the owner and publisher of the town's newspaper, was the earth: solid, steady, with a firm sense of purpose. Matt, the son of a teacher, was the wind: constantly changing his mind about who he was and what he wanted to be. Jack, the son of an unemployed alcoholic, was fire: full of angst and determination.

But one day she and Jack had found themselves alone, without Matt. They had arrived at the creek before dawn, had sat side by side, talking in their usual manner, about everything and nothing at all.

She remembered it had been an unusually warm and beautiful late-April day. Snow could still be seen on the mountains that framed Newport Falls. But in the valley, where they had been fishing, the sky was clear and the sun was bright. She had mentioned that she was getting warm and Jack had looked at her, his blue eyes sparking mischief.

He set down his pole and jumped up, pulling off his shirt. He looked at the creek, then back to her again. "You're right. A swim might be nice."

"Not *that* warm," she said. "The creek is still freezing."

"Come on. A little swim will do you good." He took a step toward her, his face lit in a devilish grin. Back then, Jack had the kind of looks sexy movie star heroes were made of: chiseled features, piercing blue eyes and jet-black hair. As she looked at him, she could feel her resolve melt. She had always had a hard time saying no to him. But, she reminded herself, this was not going to be one of those times.

"No thanks," she said. She was willing to suffer to be alone with Jack, but she was fairly certain a dip in freezing cold water would add little to their romance.

"The secret," he said, taking another step toward her, "is to jump in fast. Real fast."

She had no doubt that Jack had every intention of dropping her right into the water. Jack cared little for polite gestures. Still, he had every girl in town clamoring to be near him, for although he was a little rough and wild, he was also the most intelligent and charming boy around.

"Jack Reilly!" she said, holding her fishing pole in front of her like a sword. "Don't even think about it! I'll…I'll poke you, I will!"

He plucked the pole out of her hand and tossed it on the ground. "With what?"

She turned and ran away from the stream as fast as she could, hurdling a pile of rocks and hitting the path without losing stride. She was gaining her lead when her foot hit a stump, sending her flying over the path and into a patch of wild strawberries. Jack bounded after her, landing on his feet. He looked at her berry-splattered T-shirt. "You're hurt," he said, mistaking the red juice for blood. His tan, handsome face turned a pale white.

But as he leaned in to find the source of the "blood," she couldn't withhold her laughter any longer. She pushed him as hard as she could, sending him back on his rear. With a splat he landed smack in the berries. Then she took off running again.

But she wasn't fast enough. He grabbed her from behind. His berry-stained arms wrapped around her like two bands of steel and picked her up, but instead of carrying her off into the sunset, he began walking back toward the stream. "Let's get you cleaned up, Devonworth," he said.

"I swear, Jack," she said, trying to loosen his grip on her. "If you so much as get my little toe damp, I'll…"

"You'll what?"

They were eye-to-eye. The world once again faded away. It was just she and Jack, together. "I'll, well, I'll…"

"Idle threats," he said, his mouth so close she could feel his breath. He paused, then leaned forward as if he was about to kiss her. She closed her eyes, waiting. Maybe not so much as waiting, but willing. *Kiss me,* she thought. *Kiss me, Jack Reilly.*

But her fantasy was dashed with the rush of icy water. "Jack!" she yelled as her rear end hit the creek. When he yanked her back up, she pulled him toward her and stuck out her knee, tripping him and sending him into the cold stream.

"There's no escape," he said, pulling himself out of the water. As Katie reached the beach, Jack tackled her. He straddled her on the sand, holding her arms above her head. "Give it up, Devonworth."

Suddenly, Jack paused. He leaned over her, his eyes full of fire as he gazed at her as if for the first time. He stared at the wet T-shirt that clung to her like a second skin, revealing the shape of her breasts. "Katie," he said hoarsely.

She did what she'd been wanting to do for years: she kissed him. He responded hungrily, his tongue exploring her mouth as his hands slipped under her shirt. She could feel his raw energy press against her as his fingers gently touched her erect nipples. Although she was a virgin, she was not frightened. She wanted Jack. She needed to feel him inside her, making love to her. She was ready. Her hands clutched the top of his jeans as she fumbled for the snap.

Then, as fast as their passion flared, it banked. Jack pulled away and sat up. "What are we doing?" he asked, running his hand through his thick hair.

She was silent for a minute. Then she said, "I love you, Jack. I always have."

He didn't answer. Instead, he stood up and shoved his hands in the pockets of his wet jeans. Without saying a word, he walked away.

Katie heard a noise and turned. Matt was standing behind her, his arms crossed. She looked away, ashamed that he had witnessed such a personal humiliation.

"It's okay," Matt said. "I know you love him. I've known for a long time. Everyone has. Everyone except Jack."

Katie could still remember the terrible feeling that engulfed her. Everyone in Newport Falls knew. Knew that she suffered a case of unrequited love.

Matt held out his hand. "Come on," he said. "I'll walk you home." She accepted his hand and he pulled her to her feet. He said, "You should know that he doesn't love you. I mean, he cares about you, but not like that. He never will."

And Matt was right. Because as soon as Jack was able, he left Newport Falls.

Katie went on to college locally, and when her father died, she took over his struggling newspaper. Then she did the only sensible thing left to do: she married Matt.

"Ms. Devonworth?"

Katie snapped back to reality to see a beautiful blond woman standing in front of her. "Mr. Reilly will see you now," the woman said.

Katie felt a surge of jealousy as she wondered if the blonde was dating Jack. But so what if she was? Jack was nothing to her anymore. Nothing.

Still, her heart was pounding so loudly she was certain the woman could hear.

She walked through the open doors and into a set from *Lifestyles of the Rich and Famous.* Jack's personal office was every bit as impressive as the building. Huge, with floor-to-ceiling windows, it had a sitting area with a couch and chairs, and a meeting area with a large conference table. The center-piece of the office, however, was the elaborate, hand-carved desk that sat like a throne in front of a spectacular view of Central Park.

Jack sat at his desk, his back to her. He was facing the window, one hand behind his head as he spoke on the phone.

Being within arm's reach of him after all this time was enough to take her breath away. But apparently she had little, if any, effect on him. He appeared unaware that she was standing there, and continued talking on the phone as if she was invisible.

She stood for a few minutes, twitching her fingers nervously. Why had the secretary told her to come in if he wasn't ready? And how dare he treat her as if she was some sort of nobody! She was Katie Devonworth. She had beaten him in almost every game of chess they had ever played. She knew that he was the one who had broken Mrs. Watkins's window.

She knew that he had cried when his father had been sent to jail. She knew—

Jack spun around to face her. He smiled as he hung up the phone. He had changed little in the past nine years. His eyes may have had a few more wrinkles and his hair a few streaks of gray, but the effect was every bit as devastating as it had always been. He was still the most handsome man Katie had ever laid eyes on.

"Katie," he said, walking around the desk to greet her. He held out his hand. "It's nice to see you."

She felt a charge as he touched her. The physical connection, no matter how innocent, was enough to make her heart skip a beat. "And you," she managed to say, pulling her hand away.

"I was surprised to hear from you." His tone was chatty, as if seeing her again was the most natural thing in the world.

"Yes, well," she said, trying to match his attitude, "I was going to be in New York, anyway, so I thought, why not call Jack and see if he can meet for lunch?"

"I'm glad you did." He paused for a moment, studying her. "It's been a long time."

She shifted her gaze. What was it about him that made her act like a nervous schoolgirl?

He nodded toward the door as he grabbed his coat. "Let's go."

They walked through the lobby, pausing to retrieve her coat before heading toward the elevators. "It's all so impressive," she said, stumbling to make conversation as he helped her on with her coat.

"Thanks," he said. He pressed the button for the elevators, and they waited in silence while Katie racked her brain for something to say. Everything she came up with she rejected out of hand. *Too obvious. Too stupid. Too boring.*

When the elevator arrived, it was empty. They stepped inside, both of them keeping their eyes focused on the doors as they shut.

This was a mistake, said the voice in her head. *I can't even make small talk with him anymore. How can I ask him for a million dollars?*

"So," he said finally, "what business brings you to town?"

"Meetings with advertisers," she said, the lie just popping out of her mouth. The doors opened and several people came inside. All nodded and said hello to Jack.

"How is the paper doing?" he asked.

"Okay," she said, staring straight ahead. It wasn't exactly a lie. The reporting had never been stronger. It was the circulation that was suffering.

The elevator stopped at another floor and several more people crowded in, pushing her and Jack to the back. They were so close, their arms touching, she could smell his musky scent. She closed her eyes. For a moment she was back at the creek and Jack was on top of her, his hand caressing her breast. She could feel his tongue inside her mouth....

"Here we are," Jack said as the door opened. He put his hand on her back as he steered her out of the elevator. "I'm not sure what you had planned, but I'm afraid I don't have much time. There's a little Italian restaurant down the street, if that's all right with you."

Katie agreed. She was glad she didn't have the responsibility of picking a restaurant in a city she knew little about. They walked down the street without talking. Jack led her to a small gray building with red shutters. "This is it," he said.

They walked in and were greeted effusively by the manager, who seemed to know Jack very well. He showed them to a cozy booth in the corner. As they perused the menu, Jack said, "The chicken piccata is very good."

But Katie preferred more basic food. "How's the spaghetti and meatballs?"

"Some of the best in the city," he said. "That's what I'm getting."

"Me, too," she said, setting down her menu. As the waiter

approached, Katie wondered if conversation with her old friend was doomed to be shallow and superficial. Perhaps they no longer had anything in common but their choice of entrée.

"So," Jack said, after they had ordered, "how is everything in Newport Falls?"

"Fine," she said.

"I was so sorry to hear about your mom, Katie. She was a great person."

She wasn't expecting him to mention her mother, who had died nearly ten years ago. She had adored both Jack and Matt, and had long predicted Katie would marry one of them. When she found out she had a fatal illness, she encouraged Katie to marry quickly, so that she could attend her wedding. It was one of the main reasons Katie had agreed to marry Matt.

Fortunately, her mother had not been there to witness the demise of the marriage she had inspired. But Katie and her mother had been extremely close, and her death had left a hole in Katie's heart that would never heal. "Thank you for the flowers you sent."

"Of course," he said. He glanced away. At first she had been devastated when Jack didn't call after her mother died. But slowly the pain had given way to curiosity. Matt had a theory for Jack's disappearance from their lives. Jack had re-created himself. He didn't want anyone around who remembered him for who he was and how he had grown up.

The waitress arrived with their lunch and placed it in front of them. Plates laden with spaghetti and meatballs and the most delicious-looking garlic bread Katie had ever seen.

She picked up her fork, wondering how she was going to eat without splashing marinara sauce all over herself.

But it hadn't seemed to bother Jack. He was swirling his spaghetti on his fork and chomping away.

"What's wrong?" he asked. "Do you want something else?"

"No," she said. She stabbed her fork into the mountain of

spaghetti and popped it in her mouth. One of the noodles fell
out and, with a rather loud noise, she slurped it back in.

Jack was grinning. "No one eats like you, Devonworth."

She doubted the women Jack dated ate much of anything.
Those pictured with him in the newspapers and magazines all
looked willow thin and perfectly coiffed. *Well,* thought Katie.
I'm a real woman and proud of it. She broke her garlic bread
in half and took a big bite.

"Do you like it?" Jack asked, pointing toward her plate.

She nodded.

"There's a lot of great restaurants in the city, but there's
something about this place. It kind of reminds me of Macaroni's back home."

"It's good," she said, her mouth only half-full.

Jack grinned again.

She finished chewing and said, "But Macaroni's isn't there
anymore. They went out of business a couple of years ago."
Macaroni's wasn't the only business to fall victim to Newport
Falls' economy. Jack wouldn't recognize the once-vibrant
Main Street. Many of the stores that had been there since
Katie could remember were gone or leaving.

"Oh?" Jack said. "That's hard to believe. They'd been
there forever, hadn't they?"

"It sure seemed that way," Katie said.

Neither said anything for a while, focusing on their lunch.
But Katie couldn't relax. She knew she had to ask Jack for
money. And she had to do it soon.

Finally Jack said, "Do you ever hear from Matt?"

So Jack knew about her divorce. It didn't surprise her. The
Newport Falls grapevine ran far beyond the borders of the
city.

"Every now and then," she said. "I spoke to him last
week. He thinks he might come home soon."

"Come home?"

"He lives in the Bahamas." A marriage devoid of passion
had not been what Matt had bargained for. She hadn't loved

him, truly loved him, and he'd sensed that. She blamed herself for his philandering, blamed herself when he left town with a secretary from the bank. Their divorce had been fairly amicable. There were no property or children to dispute. They simply left the marriage with whatever they brought into it. She got the newspaper and her parents' house. He got his freedom.

Jack glanced away. "I meant, well, you said he was coming home. Does that mean returning to you?"

Katie shifted uncomfortably in her chair. She didn't want to discuss this with Jack. Not now. Not ever. "No," she said. "It means he's returning to Newport Falls. We've been divorced for almost three years now."

"I'm sorry," Jack said, his eyes meeting hers.

"Thanks. But I'm not here to discuss the failure of my marriage or my personal life." Immediately, Katie regretted her words and the tone of her voice. She didn't mean to sound so nasty. Jack had been friends with both of them. She had expected him to mention the divorce. But her feelings toward Jack and her reactions to him had never been rational.

He leaned back in the booth and crossed his arms. She could see the muscles in his jaw tighten. "All right, Devonworth," he said. "Or should I call you O'Malley?" he asked, referring to Matt's last name.

"I kept my last name. But you can call me Katie." He and Matt had always referred to each other, and her, by their last names. But they were kids then. Things had changed.

"Okay, *Katie*," he said. "Why are you here?" He wiped his mouth and put down his napkin.

She shifted her gaze. "I, uh, well, I have wondered about you. Wondered how you were doing, what you were up to…" She stumbled.

"Really?" Jack said. "You haven't asked me one question about what I've been doing. And you're doing that thing with your hair, twirling it like you do whenever you've got something on your mind."

Out of the corner of her eye she glanced at her finger. She had twisted her hair around it like a wet noodle.

Jack said, "I'm getting the impression this is more than just a personal visit."

"Okay." She lowered her hand and leaned forward. "My newspaper, *The Falls*—"

"I know the name of your newspaper."

"We're in trouble. We need cash, badly."

"I see." His blue eyes darkened. She thought he looked angry, and she guessed it was because she had not told him the truth about why she wanted to see him. "And you want me to help." It was not a question, but a statement.

"I'm hoping," she said.

Jack met her gaze directly. "What's going on?"

"We lost our major advertiser, Holland's department store."

"What happened?"

"Holland's went bankrupt last spring." Holland's was the only department store in Newport Falls. It had employed hundreds of people. A lot of those people had been forced to find work in Albany, an hour and a half south. Many had already put their homes on the market. Unfortunately, none of the real estate was selling. But that news certainly wouldn't convince Jack to invest. "But before that," she added truthfully, "circulation was growing."

"So your revenues have been increasing?"

Something about the way he asked the question told her he already knew the answer. "No," she said quietly. "I've made some changes since Dad died. I've picked up some syndicated columns and brought in some experienced reporters." She shrugged. "It all costs money."

"Money you don't have."

She swallowed. "I've already applied for loans, Jack. I've been turned down all over the place. You're my last hope. If I don't get money soon, *The Falls* is going to go out of business."

"Is that so bad? You're a terrific reporter. You could go anywhere."

"I don't want to go anywhere," she said angrily. "Newport Falls is my home. But it's not just that. My father spent his whole life working to keep this paper afloat. I've had it eleven years and I, well…" She stopped talking and took a breath. *Get a grip,* she commanded herself. *Don't start crying. This is business.* "It's not just about me," she said, meeting his eyes. "I employ almost three hundred people. Can you imagine what it will do to the local economy if *The Falls* goes out of business?"

He glanced away.

She could still read Jack Reilly like a book. And her instincts told her that coming here was a waste of time. He had no interest in investing in a small-town newspaper that would never make a lot of money.

He shook his head. "I'm sorry, Devonworth," he began. "I mean," he said quickly, "Katie."

"Please, Jack," she said. "We were friends once. I need your help."

Jack looked at her. He hesitated. As if on cue, his phone rang, giving him the distraction he no doubt wanted. From what he said, she could tell he was talking to someone at his office. Then she heard him say, "What's on my schedule tomorrow?" He paused, looked at Katie and said, "Cancel it. I have to go out of town. Arrange a trip to Newport Falls. It's outside of Albany, that's where. Thanks." He hung up the phone and said to Katie, "I want to go there and see it."

"What?" she asked.

"Your paper, of course. *The Falls.*"

Jack had been inside the building a million times when they were growing up. Besides a new coat of paint, nothing had changed.

He continued, "I want to meet some of these hotshot reporters you've hired. I want to talk to your director of advertising and see how firm his—"

"Her," she corrected him.

"Her commitments are for the next couple of years. See what she's doing to increase revenues."

"Okay," she said.

He stood up. "I'll be at your office at three."

When he held out his hand, she took it and stood. But he didn't let go immediately. She thought he held on for a split second too long as he said, "It's good to see you again, Katie."

Jack escorted Katie to the corner and hailed her a cab. After she was seated, she turned up her face to him and said, "Thanks, Jack." He tried not to focus on her soft, red lips; instead, he shut the door. But he stood there, watching the cab pull away. Only after it disappeared from sight did he finally move—and then not back to his office but in the opposite direction.

He needed a chance to clear his mind. Seeing Katie again, being so close to her after all these years, made his head spin.

He'd always hoped that he had been successful in his attempt to rid her from his mind. But he had found just because he'd taken her out of his life did not mean her spirit no longer lingered. She was the standard that he challenged other women to meet, she was the ghost with whom they competed.

When she first called him, he'd told himself that it would be harmless to meet with her. She no longer had any power over him. But when she walked into his office that afternoon all hopes of being over Katie Devonworth faded. The girl of his dreams had turned into a woman, more beautiful than he could imagine. Her chestnut hair had been cut to her shoulders, framing her big brown expressive eyes. She was as slim and athletic as she had been in high school, but now with curves in all the right places. The blouse she'd worn had clung to her breasts, allowing him to see their fullness.

From the moment he saw her, he knew that he would have to make their lunch as short as possible. That he would have to endure his time with her and then do his best to forget her again. He had little choice. Katie had made it clear long ago that she no longer loved him.

Once again, he thought of that moment at the creek, the day she confessed her feelings for him. He could still remember the taste of her lips, the smell of her skin.

He had loved Katie more than life itself, and it had taken every ounce of conviction to walk away from her. But he had little choice. He knew only too well what happened when love was consummated too soon. He himself was the result of such a liaison.

When he first met Jack's mother, his father, Robert, had been nineteen, a college freshman in the small town of Addison Park, Iowa. His mother, June, was only sixteen, still in high school. They fell in love at first sight and quickly became inseparable. They pledged their love, determined to spend the rest of their lives together. But June's parents were not pleased with the match. They had hoped their only daughter would do better than an orphan dependent on scholarships. When June got pregnant, Robert begged her parents to allow them to marry. But her parents wouldn't consider it. Embarrassed by their daughter's pregnancy, they sent her away without telling his father where she'd gone. Robert had found out too late that she had been sent to live with an aunt in the country.

His father never saw his mother again. When his mother went into labor, her aunt had tried to deliver the baby herself. June had died in childbirth. His father had taken Jack and returned home to Newport Falls, but he'd never forgiven himself.

Jack was reminded of his parents' doomed relationship every day of his life. He vowed that no matter how much he loved Katie, no matter how much he desired her, he would not allow her to suffer the same fate as his mother. He needed to become the type of man Katie deserved; then, and only then, would they have a future.

Jack left for college determined to prove himself, determined to make something of himself. And when he did, only when he did, would he be able to marry the woman he loved.

But he had misjudged the situation. He had convinced himself that he and Katie had a special connection, a connection that didn't need to be spoken of to be real.

But he was wrong. Just when he had begun to make something of himself and felt ready to propose, she had married his best friend.

The marriage had shocked him. How could she? If she had felt for him one tenth of what he did, she would never have been able to escape into someone else's arms.

And Matt? Matt wasn't interested in Katie until he found out how Jack felt about her. He remembered the night in junior high when he told Matt he loved her. They were lying in Old Man Kroner's field, arms crossed, looking up at the sky. Just the two of them. Matt had been teasing him about some girl in school when Jack told him he had it all wrong.

"What do you mean?" Matt had asked.

"I mean," Jack said, "that I love someone else."

Matt rolled over. *Love* was a big word, and being in tenth grade, neither had ever used it to describe a feeling before. "You?" Matt asked. "Who?"

"Katie," Jack said. "I'm going to marry her one day."

"Katie?" Matt laughed. "Oh, right!"

"What's so funny? I have it all figured out. I even have the ring."

"Where did you get it? A Cracker Jack box?"

"It was my grandmother's. My father wanted to give it to my mother, but he never got a chance. It's a diamond, with two rubies on either side—"

"Wait a minute," Matt interrupted. "Katie is someone you play basketball with. She's not the type of girl you fall in love with. And marry? Come on!"

"She's who I want," Jack said. "Who I've always wanted."

Matt fell silent again. Then he said, "Does she know?"

"No. I can't tell her yet. Not now."

"Why not?"

"Because we're too young. Katie and I aren't going to end up like my parents."

Matt was silent.

"I have to wait," Jack said. "I have a plan. I'm going to make a million dollars and then I'll marry her."

"If you make a million dollars there's gonna be a lot of women you can marry."

"I don't want a lot of women. I want Katie."

Jack should've known that Matt would then want her, too. Matt had always competed with him. Jack never understood it. After all, his friend had such a head start in life. He came from a good family, was a natural athlete, went to all the best schools. Yet he always seemed to be looking over his shoulder at Jack.

Shortly before Jack returned from Europe, he had called Matt. He was worried about Katie. Her father's death had been extremely hard on her, and she'd had to leave college to take over the reins of his struggling newspaper. Jack couldn't stand to be so far from her, knowing that she was in pain and not being there to provide comfort. So even though he had not yet acquired the financial position he'd hoped, he could no longer wait to propose to Katie. He was coming home. It was time to tell Katie how much he loved her and ask for her hand in marriage.

Matt, his best friend, had betrayed him, rushing forward with his own proposal. He and Katie were married the day Jack returned. Jack had attended their wedding with his grandmother's ring still in his pocket.

But it was not a clear victory. On the day of the wedding, right after Matt had gloated over his "win," he had asked Jack to stay away from her. To break off contact. "You'll only confuse her," Matt had said.

"Confuse her?" Jack had asked. "What are you talking about? I thought you said she loves you."

"She married me, didn't she?" Matt had said, before walking away. But Matt needn't have worried. Jack could no longer stand to be around Katie. Even when he heard about their divorce, he convinced himself that it was best not to call her. Still, he'd hoped she might call and tell him she'd made a mistake marrying Matt. That it was he she had loved all along, not Matt. But the call never came. And so he Jack attempted to exorcise her from his mind and his life. He had no choice. His love for her was poisoning him and his relationships with other women.

But today she reappeared, asking for help. And he realized immediately why he had never called her. He couldn't. His love for her was every bit as strong as it had been that day down by the creek. But unlike that day, it was unrequited.

Jack found himself stopped in front of his office. Still, he thought, looking up at the towering building that bore his name, he owed Katie. Because if it were not for her, he doubted he would've been able to channel so much fire and energy into his work. He would never have succeeded.

And so he would try to help her. He'd give her a chance, but that was all.

He'd go to Newport Falls, as promised. It was only a day, eight hours max. He could handle being back in Newport Falls, being with Katie, for a day. Especially now. After landing an international deal, he was moving to London in several weeks to open a European branch of his company.

Once again, he thought of the day at the creek, the day that Katie had said she loved him. How intoxicating it had been.

He should've known that chances of a lifetime don't come twice.

Two

"**D**on't read too much into it," Marcella warned her. Marcella was the director of advertising for *The Falls*, as well as Katie's friend. "He said it was good to see you. I'm sure he meant it."

"What makes you think I'm reading too much into it?" Katie asked. After a fitful night, she'd arrived at the office at 5:00 a.m., pulling files and getting everything ready for Jack's visit. To make matters worse, Matt had called and she'd made the mistake of telling him about seeing Jack. Surprisingly, he had morphed into the big brother once again, warning her to be careful. But careful of what?

"Because of the look in your eyes whenever you mention his name."

Katie thought of Matt's admonition. Was this what he'd insinuated? That despite her marriage and the years that had passed, she was still in love with his former best friend? "What look?"

"The he's-so-dreamy look."

"The man every gossip columnist refers to as the Iceman?"

"I thought it was Heartbreak Kid," Marcella retorted.

Katie nodded. Jack was a constant figure in the society columns across the country. He was a known playboy, beloved by gossips everywhere.

She shook her head and sighed. "He sure didn't act as if he was happy to see me. He was so…distant. He didn't even talk to me directly when I called. And he kept me waiting for forty-five minutes—"

"And then he offered to bail you out."

"He didn't offer. Not yet, anyway. He wants to see me jump through hoops first. And even then, there are no guarantees."

Marcella shrugged. That was all Katie needed to keep going. She said, "It *is* nice of him to come all the way out here, but I had to beg him to help. And I can guarantee you he's not excited about it. You should have seen him at lunch. It was obvious he doesn't want anything to do with me anymore."

"Like I said, you're reading too much into this."

"Am I? He made me wait and then he kept me twiddling my thumbs while he ignored me. He never even bothered to apologize. I knew he would be late today." She pointed to her watch. "It's four o'clock."

"But his office said his morning meeting ran a little longer than expected."

"It's all part of his schtick."

"What schtick?"

"The I'm-a-big-deal-now schtick." Like most of the people who worked for her, Katie had known Marcella her whole life. They'd gone to school together, and Marcella had not only witnessed Katie's crush on Jack but had seen how devastated Katie had been when Jack hadn't reciprocated her feelings.

"He *is* a big deal. And he's giving you a chance. That's more than any of the other people would do."

"Humph." Katie shrugged.

"Maybe there are some unresolved feelings."

"No way. If he still cared a hoot about me he would've called or written."

"I wasn't talking about Jack."

Katie stared up from her desk. "I may have cared for the old Jack Reilly, the one without the fancy suits and high-rise office, but I couldn't care less about the new version. He's not my type."

"He was for a very long time."

"That was before he left town, before he stopped writing, stopped calling. Before he forgot who he was."

"I think thou dost protest too much."

Katie felt her cheeks heating up. "I guarantee you, whatever feelings I had for Jack Reilly are no more. Sure, he may still make me nervous," she said, remembering the way her heart had accelerated when she first saw him again, "but that's normal."

Marcella raised her eyebrows.

"My interest in Jack Reilly is purely professional. I called him only as a last resort. I mean, wait till he gets here. You'll see. It's no accident that we've had to wait a gazillion minutes. Jack's so cocky now, so arrogant, so full of himself..."

"And so behind you," Marcella said.

Jack stood in the doorway. He'd heard almost every word of Katie's litany against him. But it hadn't angered him. In fact, he was flattered he could still squeak genuine emotion out of the normally reserved town sweetheart.

"I'm sorry I'm late," he said. "My meeting ran a little long this morning."

He pretended not to notice the look of absolute horror in Katie's eyes. He saw her glance at Marcella. "No problem," Katie said quickly.

"And then my pilot had some last-minute things to take care of before we took off."

"*My* pilot?" asked Marcella. She shot Katie a look, impressed. "You have your own plane?"

Jack nodded. "Anyway, I can see I'm interrupting. I'd be happy to wait, though. How long do you think you'll be? A gazillion minutes?"

"Nice to see you again, Jack," Marcella said, rushing past him.

"Look, Jack," Katie said. Her normally pale face was beet red. "I'm sorry about that. You know me. I never liked to wait."

Jack's smile faded. "Yes," he said. She certainly had not waited for him. "I know."

"Well," she said, breezing past him. Jack recognized her perfume. It was soft yet enticing, the same scent she'd worn in high school. She turned to face him. Then she flashed him the smile he had committed to memory. "Let's get started, shall we?"

Katie had the sudden urge to throw up. How could she have been so stupid, talking about him like that when he was due any time? Whatever her history was with Jack, she had to get over it. After all, she needed him. This paper needed him. Without him, the entire town was sunk.

But still… She thought of the way he'd mentioned his pilot. It was as if he wanted her to know that he didn't fly commercial anymore. He had his own private plane. Well, big deal! He may be a hotshot in New York, but she would always be able to cream him with a snowball.

She showed Jack around the offices. He seemed unimpressed, almost bored. He sat through the various meetings with a stone face, every now and then interrupting to ask a question.

At one point, when she and Marcella escaped to the ladies' room, Marcella grabbed her arm and said, "Oh, my God, he's so gorgeous…I mean, he was always gorgeous but not like that. What happened to him?''

''It's the suit,'' Katie replied, trying to convince herself. And they both laughed. For it was apparent that underneath the expensive suit, the crisp, starched shirt and the pearl cuff links, Jack was every bit the muscular hunk he had been in school.

At the end of the day, she led him back to her office. ''I'd like to meet with some of those reporters you talked about,'' he said.

''Right,'' Katie replied. She picked up her phone and dialed Luanna Combs, her most recent coup. Luanna had worked at the *Baltimore Sun* for ten years before joining *The Falls*. But Luanna didn't pick up her extension.

Katie hung up the phone, distressed. She checked her watch. It was almost six. Except for today she wouldn't expect Luanna to be at the office past five-thirty. After all, that was part of the deal, part of why she was able to woo high-level staff. She promised flexible work hours and little overtime, a family-friendly environment.

She glanced at Jack. He crossed his arms.

She swallowed and tried another extension. Bobby, the assistant for the reporters, picked up. ''Where's Luanna?'' she asked.

''She left. Said she was really sorry, but she got a call from school. Her kid's got red spots all over—they think it's chicken pox.''

''What about Brett?'' she asked. Brett Wilson was her top reporter, whom she'd somehow snagged from the *Los Angeles Times*.

''Tanker overturned on Route 44. Brett's covering it.''

''And Shelley?'' she asked, already anticipating the answer.

''Gone. Her husband got the stomach flu so she had to pick up her kids from day care. Turned in her story, though. Damn good.''

When she hung up the phone, Jack raised his eyebrows and said, ''Well?''

"They're not here."

"None of them? Where are they?"

"The three I wanted you to meet aren't... Well, they're not available right now."

"This newspaper's future is riding on three employees? That's why you haven't increased revenues? Because you're paying top dollar to only three—"

"They'll be in tomorrow," she said crossly. "If you can't stick around to talk to them, well, I guess I'll just thank you for your time and see you out."

He hesitated a moment. "They'll be *available* tomorrow—guaranteed?"

"Guaranteed," she said. Even if she had to watch their kids for them and cover the newsbeat.

"Okay," he said.

"You'll stay?" she asked, surprised.

He nodded as he flipped open his cell phone and called his office. She could hear him talking to his secretary, rearranging his schedule. "And call Carol," he said. "See if you can reschedule her for another night."

Jealousy stabbed her heart. Carol? He was obviously canceling a date.

She cleared her throat, as if trying to rid herself of poisonous feelings. She had no business being jealous. Instead, she should be feeling sorry for the poor woman. After all, he didn't even have the decency to call himself, his secretary did it for him.

He shut the phone and told her, "One more day." He looked at his watch. "Does Mrs. Crutchfield still run the inn on Main Street?"

"Yep," Katie said. But she didn't see this new Jack Reilly comfortable in a simple country inn. She was certain he would prefer accommodations that offered room service. "But there's a nice Hyatt in Albany."

"The inn will be fine. I'll ask Greg to drive some clothes over."

"Who's Greg and what clothes?"

"Greg's my pilot. He does a bunch of things besides just flying planes."

"You mean he's a valet, too?" She couldn't help the sarcasm.

Once again, she saw the grin creep up his lips. "If needed. I keep an extra set of clothes on the plane, just in case."

"Of course," she said. After all, who didn't?

When she stood up, Jack surprised her and said, "Do you have plans this evening?"

"I, uh, no," she stammered.

"Good. I'd like to take you out to a nice dinner. Pick any place you want. We can catch up."

"Sure," she said. She had just the place in mind.

Joe's Diner was located on the corner of Main and Howe Streets, almost directly across the street from the paper. It had been in existence ever since Joe Pecorillo first arrived in Albany from Italy in the late 1920s. Since then, it had stayed in the family, passing from Joe Sr., to Joe Jr., to Joe the third. Joe the third, otherwise known as Joey, was about sixty years old and had managed it since Katie was a kid. She, Jack and Matt had spent many hours at Joe's sharing milkshakes and burgers. Jack even worked there his senior year before college.

If Jack was surprised by her choice, he didn't show it. In fact, she thought he seemed relieved, almost happy that she had not chosen a more romantic and quiet place.

After Jack had shaken hands with Joe they settled into a worn, yet cozy booth by the window. Jack looked around and said, "It's kind of quiet for Thursday night, isn't it?"

Besides them, only three other tables were taken. "Not really," she said. "I told you, things have changed. I'm sure you noticed the out-of-business signs. A lot of people have left town. It's hard to find work around here. Unless something is done, Newport Falls is going to turn into a ghost town."

"But Lois Lane is going to save it. Or do you see yourself as Brenda Starr?"

"Neither," she said coldly. "This is my hometown. I love it here. I love the fact that when I'm sick, I can count on Mrs. Crutchfield to make me chicken soup. I can count on Ms. Faunally to bring me her homemade strawberry jelly in the spring. I can count on the Wellers to entertain the entire town at Halloween. I can count on Mr. Pete to know I'm entertaining if I buy an extra package of steaks at his grocery store. I can count on the wild azaleas to bloom like crazy every summer. I know some people don't like small towns, but—"

"You do. I got it, Devonworth. But not everyone has such fond memories of this place."

She stopped. Jack's father had died the year after he left for college. They had buried him in the town cemetery, not too far from where her parents were buried. "I know," she said. "But your memories aren't all bad, are they?"

"No. Thanks to you…and Matt," he said, adding Matt's name almost as an afterthought.

"Lots of other people cared about you, too," Katie said. "Lots of other people still do. Mr. Pete was just asking me about you the other day."

"How's his business?" Jack asked. He had worked for Mr. Pete for years, bagging groceries and helping out around the store.

"Like everything else, not great."

"I'm sorry to hear that," Jack said. Then without skipping a beat he said, "Should we order?"

Katie ate her meal in silence, inwardly steaming about the cold, callous way Jack had handled the news of Mr. Pete's business. How could he be so offhand about a man who had been nothing but kind to him? After they finished eating, she said, "Do you plan on seeing anyone else while you're here?"

He stood up and took her coat off the hook, held it open for her. "No."

"No?" she repeated as she slipped into her coat. "I'm sure Mrs. Bayons would like to see you."

"I don't have time," he said.

"Maybe tomorrow—"

"No. I have something to take care of in the morning. After which I'm going directly to your office. I have to be back in the city tomorrow night."

"Oh, right." For his date with Carol.

"I doubt I have anything to say to anyone here, anyway."

His aim had been direct and sharp. She stopped walking and looked at him, hurt. She got the message. Jack had broken all connection to Newport Falls.

But Jack appeared oblivious to her pain. He said goodbye to Joe and held the door open for her. "Come on," he said. "I'll walk you to your car."

But she didn't have a car. This morning, despite the fact that it was January and freezing cold, she had ridden her bike. She told Jack.

He looked at her, surprised. "You rode your bike in this weather?"

"Why not? The roads are clear. Besides, I wanted exercise."

"You're not still living at your parents' place, are you?"

Her parents' farm was about five miles outside of town. More than a hundred acres, it included an old and rather worn Victorian house and a pond where they had fished and swum in the summers, ice-skated in the winters. "I've moved back there, yes."

"It's too far and too cold to ride all the way back. I'll drive you. I rented a car at the airport."

But she didn't think she could stand one more minute talking to him or not talking to him, as the case might be. What had happened to her friend? To the warm, caring, funny guy whom she had loved with all of her heart?

Outside the newspaper, she stopped at the bike rack on the sidewalk. There was no lock on her bike, none was needed in Newport Falls. "Thanks for dinner," she said. She felt a raindrop, then another. No matter, she was used to riding in all types of weather.

Jack grabbed her hand and stopped her. He hesitated a moment and then said, "You can't save the world, Devonworth."

"I don't want to save the world, Reilly. Just Newport Falls."

He held tight, pulling her back toward him. "I can't let you go like this."

"Why not?" she asked, her heart pounding.

"Because," he said, dropping her hand and motioning toward the sky, "it's raining."

She pulled her sneakers out of her backpack. "You used to ride your bike in the rain all the time," she replied as she switched shoes right there on the sidewalk. "Or did you forget about that, too?" When she was finished, she shoved her pumps into her bag and hopped on her bike as gracefully as she could. "See you tomorrow."

She pedaled through the dark streets. She knew each and every home by heart. They were inhabited by friends, by people she had known her entire life. As she drove by the yellow bungalow on the corner, she knew that the blue light flickering on the first floor meant Mr. and Mrs. Holmes were sitting in their matching La-Z-Boys, watching *Jeopardy* on the living-room TV. She pedaled past old Mrs. Honeywell's house. She knew the dim light in the second-floor window meant Mrs. Honeywell was tucked into bed, petting her white poodle, Betsy, and reading one of the bloody mysteries she was so fond of. She passed by the little red house on the corner. The house was dark because its owners, Jan and Tony Bintlif, and their newborn son, Alex, were visiting Jan's parents in Florida.

She was glad it was raining, because if anyone saw her in the dark gloom of this January night, they wouldn't notice her tears. Jack was right about one thing: she desperately wanted to save Newport Falls. She would never again find a place where everyone knew not only her first and last name, but her middle name, as well. A place where people didn't have to worry about locking their doors. A place where *stranger* was a foreign word.

Unfortunately, Marcella was right. Katie wouldn't be able to save the town without Jack's help.

When headlights flashed behind her, Katie rode over to the side of the road. But the car didn't pass. Instead, it pulled up alongside her. "You sure you don't want a ride?" It was Jack.

"I'm sure," she said. "Good night."

He slowed the car down, and for a minute she thought he was going to turn around. But he didn't. He followed behind her, his headlights illuminating the way.

Jack followed her all the way home. He pulled his car into her driveway, parking behind her. He knew she was annoyed but he didn't care. He wasn't about to let her ride her bike on a rainy night alone. It made no difference that Newport Falls was the safest place in the country. The roads were slick and a tired driver might not notice someone pedaling a bike on the side of the road. After all, who in their right mind would ride a bike to work in January?

Katie, of course. She had always done things differently from anyone else. Eccentric, they'd call her in New York City. There had never been, nor would there ever be, another woman like her. Feisty and opinionated, beautiful and brainy, with a killer body and a heart of gold.

When Katie tapped on his window, he rolled it down. "You didn't need to follow me home," she said.

"What?" he said, pretending to be surprised. "I thought this was the way to the inn!" The inn, which everyone knew, was directly next to the diner.

Katie grinned. It was enough to make him smile. He nodded toward her parents' house. "It still looks the same."

Katie nodded. "Thanks for following me," she said. "I

guess I'll see you tomorrow.'' Then she bounded off toward the house.

Part of him wanted to chase after her. Open a bottle of wine and sit by the fire, just the two of them. He would tell her how nice it was to see her again. Explain how badly he felt that they had lost contact. How he wanted to make things right…

He stopped himself. He could not allow old feelings to surface. He reminded himself once again that Katie had long ago stopped caring for him, and only a fool would think otherwise. As he had heard her say in her office, she had turned to him only as a last resort. And it was only for money.

But her heart was in the right place. He could see why she was attached to Newport Falls, and he knew why she was desperate to save it. How it had changed since he had grown up here! There was a distinct creakiness to the town now, as if it were suffering from a terminal illness. The changes were not subtle. For Sale signs littering yards. Stores with windows boarded up. Empty streets and restaurants. It made him sad to think that Newport Falls might soon be just as Katie had said. A ghost town.

Jack drove back to the inn, mulling over all the thoughts that cluttered his mind. He didn't like feeling this way, his mind in turmoil. He found himself yearning to be back in the safe, sterile confines of his office. His life had a comfortable rhythm, revolving around work. There were women, of course. Plenty of women. But his relationships were based on sex, not emotion.

But the gossip columnists were wrong when they said he did not want to commit. He was envious of his peers with wives and families. He could only hope he would be so lucky one day. But first, he needed to find the right woman.

And to forget about Katie.

Three

Katie woke up the next morning feeling as if she had just dodged a bullet. She was surprised by her feelings for Jack. She had hoped that their years apart would've lessened her desire for him, that she was finally over him.

For a while at least, she had half convinced herself she had succeeded. After all, it had been so awkward in the diner. It hadn't seemed as strange being with Jack in New York. But to be having dinner with the man she had loved so intensely, in the place where they had spent so much time, was odd and uncomfortable, to say the least. He had changed since they were last at Joe's Diner. Jack was still handsome, there was no doubt about that. But it wasn't his looks that had attracted Katie. It was his heart.

But just when she was certain that he had hardened over the years, that her friend was unrecognizable, he went and followed her home. Sweet and a little crazy, it was a total Jack thing to do.

Thankfully she had possessed enough self-control and self-respect not to invite him in. After all, the end result would have been disastrous. She probably would've confessed her true feelings or, worse yet, acted on them. And Jack, once again, would've run for the hills. She would have been left brokenhearted all over again. And she would've let down all the people who worked for her. All the people who were dependent upon Jack investing in *The Falls*.

Damn! She had half hoped that Jack really had changed. That his tough childhood had finally caught up with him and he'd lost the sweetness he had once preserved so effortlessly. It would have been understandable. After all, despite his recent success, life had given him many reasons to be bitter. He'd never known his mother, nor had he known any other relatives besides his father. And although Katie had always felt Jack's father loved him, he was too incapacitated to function as a parent. Jack had grown up in a one-bedroom shack on the outskirts of town. Many times the house had no running water or heat. But Jack never grieved over his situation. He'd worked as long as Katie could remember, paying for his own clothes and groceries. He raised not only himself, but took care of his father, as well.

There was no self-pity, either. "There're a lot of people who have it worse than me," he'd said whenever she or Matt would express concern. And that may have been true. One thing was certain, though. No one in Newport Falls had it worse than Jack Reilly.

And, because of that, Jack always had to fight for respect. There were a couple of incidents in which Jack was blamed for something he didn't do—like when the tools were stolen from the hardware store and the time someone robbed the Creeley house. But in both instances Jack was exonerated. It seemed like some people just couldn't believe a boy who had grown up with a rotten father could be so decent and kind. But he was.

Katie remembered the spring day she, Matt and Jack were walking home from school and saw black smoke billowing out of the Pelton home. Mrs. Pelton was crying on the street, comforting her six-year-old son, Frank. "They're still in-side," the boy was screaming. "Rosie's still inside."

Rosie was the family dog, a four-year-old golden retriever who had just had puppies. A normally obedient dog, Rosie had sensed danger and refused to leave her babies. Mrs. Pel-ton and Frank had run out of the house, narrowly escaping, but the dogs were trapped in the boy's second-floor bedroom.

Before Katie could stop him, Jack had climbed the tree in front of the Pelton home. He jumped from the tree to the roof, just as he had done at her house many times. When he tried to open the window and found it locked, he kicked it in, shattering the glass. He pulled his T-shirt up over his mouth and climbed inside.

Both Katie and Matt had pleaded with him to stay outside with them. But when it became apparent Jack wasn't going to listen, Matt followed him up the tree.

Suddenly, Jack appeared at the window with a puppy in his hands. One at a time he handed them to Matt, who passed them down to Katie. When all four puppies were rescued, Jack appeared with Rosie. They escaped just as the flames licked the window. By the time the fire trucks arrived, the house was destroyed.

Jack became a local hero after that. The town even gave him a special award at a picnic in his honor. But his father didn't show. The night of the picnic Katie could see Jack looking around for him. Afterward, when she mentioned it, he had blown it off in his typical casual manner. "It's no big deal," he said. "I didn't expect him to be there." But she knew whether he expected him or not, it still hurt. "You guys were there," he said. "That's what counts."

She always knew Jack would leave town as soon as he could. She wasn't surprised when he got a full academic scholarship to Princeton. Nor was she surprised when he chose prestigious summer internships over bagging groceries in Newport Falls. Although she told herself that it was the logical thing to do, her heart still ached. She missed Jack, longed for him. And she held on to the hope that one day he would feel the same way about her.

But each year he wrote less and less. She and Matt found themselves comparing notes, trying to read between the lines in Jack's abbreviated letters. Although he returned when her father died and stayed with her for an entire week, it was clear their relationship had run its course. When Jack graduated from college and took a position in London, Katie couldn't hide her devastation. She knew that even though he said when he returned, things would be as they once were between them, his promise was an empty one. Their friendship was all but over.

With Jack in Europe and her father gone, Katie had relied more than ever on her old friend Matt. Everyone had assumed she and Matt were a couple long before it had occurred to Katie. She had just never seen Matt that way. But when her mother became ill and jumped on the bandwagon, as well, Katie had forced herself to see him as a potential candidate for romance.

Still, Katie held out for Jack. Then one day Matt informed her that Jack was the one who had encouraged him to ask her out in the first place. Matt told her that Jack had always known the two of them were meant for each other. That Jack had even encouraged him to marry her.

Katie had been stunned. But then she thought back to the day at the creek, and it all seemed to make sense. Jack had never loved her. If he had, he wouldn't have left.

As Katie recalled those days so long ago, she poured herself a cup of coffee and curled up on the living-room couch. She remembered that when she had decided to marry Matt, she'd told herself she was making a wise decision. She would be with her friend, her best friend, the remainder of her life. It was the only way to assure that he wouldn't leave her, too, that she wouldn't suffer another heartbreak.

But, of course, she had. Marriage was no insurance against pain.

Theirs had lasted only six years. She had cut him free, just as he had wished. Not only had she given him his freedom, she had forgiven him.

She realized that she had not extended the same courtesy to Jack. As much as she tried, her heart had never let him go. She had hung on to her feelings like a sole survivor on a sinking ship. She needed to let him go, finally and forever.

She was embarrassed by her behavior the previous evening. Jack had come to Newport Falls to try to help her, yet she had returned his kindness by behaving like a spurned lover.

Katie set down her coffee. She was thankful to have another day with her old friend. She would apologize to Jack and make it up to him. Glancing at her watch, she saw it was almost eight. Jack said he had some business to take care of before heading to the office. And she knew just where to find him.

Jack walked through the arched gates of the cemetery, carrying three bouquets of red roses. The temperature had dropped sharply and the rain had turned to snow. Several inches were already on the ground. Jack glanced around, admiring the familiar landscape. The cemetery seemed to be the only place in Newport Falls that was just as he remembered. Beautiful, yet desolate.

He stepped over the withered, barren rosebushes and made his way over to where his father was buried. Jack had been here several times to pay respects, though the visits were never pleasant. It wasn't just his father's death that saddened him, but his life. His father had been an alcoholic for as long as Jack could remember. His life had been a graveyard of missed opportunities.

Jack's father had never recovered from the loss of the woman he loved so dearly. He tried at first, attempting to reclaim his sanity by dropping out of college and returning to Newport Falls. But even old friends couldn't save him from the guilt. Stalked by invisible demons, he found solace only in alcohol. Jack couldn't remember a time when his father was employed. Nor could he remember his father ever showing any tenderness toward him. Jack had grown up fast, forced to fend not only for himself, but many times, for his father, as well. Jack had been determined to make the town proud of him, determined that his fate would be different than his father's. He wouldn't allow himself to be destroyed by love. But it seemed the harder he tried to escape, the more furiously fate pursued him.

When Katie had married Matt, Jack had found escape from his pain not through the bottle, but work. He went to Yale for his MBA. He was willing to work longer, harder than anyone else. And his determination paid off. In a business built on family contacts, Jack climbed his way up the ladder the old-fashioned way, rung by rung.

Jack wished he had known his father better. He wished he could talk to him, tell him that he now understood the pain. He now understood why his father shut himself off from the world. Shut himself off from his only child.

Jack placed one bouquet of red roses on his father's grave and stood up, brushing the snow off his pants. But he wasn't ready to leave. He walked toward the old oak tree where the Devonworths were buried.

At first he had trouble finding their graves. The snow was falling faster now, sticking to the ground in fat, white clumps. But he persevered, brushing the snow off the tombstones until he found their matching white ones. Jack had known they would not have anything elaborate, anything that drew attention to the spot. They were plain, simple people in life, and he knew that was the way they wanted to be remembered.

As Jack placed the remaining roses on their grave, he felt a rush of emotion. The Devonworths always stood behind him. No matter what was happening at home, he could always count on them for support. They had welcomed him into their home for meals and holidays, always treating him with love and respect.

He would've liked to repay their kindness. To promise them that he would do his best to take care of their daughter. But it was too late for promises.

He turned to leave. He had a terrible task to deal with today. On some level he had known from the moment Katie had asked him for money that his company could not invest. Yet he had convinced himself that perhaps things had changed, perhaps *The Falls* was not the simple paper he remembered. He'd been kidding himself, and instead of just leaving after his meetings yesterday, he had extended his visit. Why? Because of some lingering sentiment toward Katie. But he couldn't help her. He doubted anyone could. It didn't matter what reporters she had working for her. It didn't matter how many awards they won or what syndicated columns Katie could pick up.

A paper in a dying town was a losing investment.

"Jack?"

At first he thought he was imagining things. But there she was, underneath the cemetery's arched gates. "Katie," he breathed.

She walked toward him. Snowflakes had attached to her long lashes. The ends of her red scarf, wrapped around her slender neck, blew sideways in the wind. "What are you doing here?" he asked.

"I wanted to talk to you. Away from the office."

"But how did you know I'd be here?"

"You haven't been back in years. What other business could you possibly have?"

He smiled. "Good work, detective."

He glanced at the entranceway, and his smile evaporated as he recognized Katie's bike parked outside. The thought of her riding her bike five miles in a snowstorm was like an ice pick going through his heart. He asked, "What was so important that it couldn't wait?"

"I needed to apologize. You came back here to help me and I've had a chip on my shoulder ever since you arrived."

Once again Jack thought of her parents buried behind him. Katie had lost her parents, her husband, and was about to lose the only other thing that mattered to her—her paper. She had been dealing with this all alone because he had hung her out to dry. "Don't be ridiculous," he said.

"I'm sorry." She looked at him and her eyes welled with tears. Instinct took over and he wrapped his arms around her. "Hey," he said, "it's me, Jack. There's no need for apologies. I'm the one who owes you an apology."

She seemed so light, almost ethereal. He wanted to hold her and protect her from the world. Suddenly, he didn't think he could ever let go.

But Katie seemed to feel differently. She stiffened slightly, as if uncomfortable with his touch. He dropped his arms, and she stepped back from him.

He couldn't blame her. What kind of a friend had he been? "You have every reason to be angry with me."

"What do you mean?"

"I should've come back for your mother's funeral. I'm sorry. And I should've called when I heard you and Matt were getting divorced."

"I don't blame you," she said. She shrugged and tucked her gloved hands in her pockets. "You were busy."

"No," Jack said. "That's no excuse. It was… There were other reasons." Selfish ones, he wanted to say. He could not forgive her for marrying Matt.

Katie glanced down at the ground. "I know it's hard for you to come back here," she said. "If I was you, I don't know if I would want to come back to Newport Falls, either. I just… Well, I know your dad was very proud of you, Jack. He loved you." Her eyes met his. "And so did…everyone else."

"Your parents were always kind to me," he said.

At the mention of her mother and father, she glanced toward the old oak tree. She could see the red flowers already dusted with snow. Surprised, she said, "You brought flowers?"

Jack nodded.

Still looking at her parents' graves, she said, "I'm almost

glad they're not here to see what's happening to the paper. It would break their hearts."

What would break their hearts, Jack thought, was their daughter's unhappiness. Jack took a step toward her, reaching out a gloved hand to touch her face.

This time she did not move away. Her eyes closed and her head seemed to melt into his hand. She touched his fingers, holding them to her cheek. Desire for her flooded his every muscle and vein. This is Katie, he reminded himself. She married your best friend....

She lifted her head slightly. For once, Jack ignored the voice in his head. His need for her was too overwhelming.

He crashed back through time. She was Katie, his Katie, and she was close enough to kiss. He leaned forward.

Just then, her bicycle fell, clanging against the steel gate of the cemetery. Jack jumped, like a thief caught approaching a vault.

Katie stood still, staring at him with her big brown eyes.

What in the hell was he doing? Had he lost his mind? Katie shows a little kindness and he's ready to jump in the sack?

Because that was all it was. Wasn't it? He wasn't interested in anything more than a physical relationship. As he always joked, he was already married—to his job. He didn't have the time nor the desire to fall in love.

Especially with Katie. He had already made that mistake.

Jack cleared his throat. One thing was clear. He needed to take care of business and get the hell out. Before he did something he regretted. He turned and walked over to her bike. With one hand, he lifted it to his shoulder and nodded toward his car. "We better get back to your office if I'm going to meet with those reporters." He glanced at his watch. "I only have a little bit of time before I have to leave." He didn't trust himself to be around Katie Devonworth any longer than necessary.

Four

Katie looked across the table where her three top reporters, Luanna, Shelley and Brett, were finishing up summaries of their résumés and the type of stories they specialized in.

She glanced over at Jack. He was sitting next to her, his eyes focused on her reporters. Her thoughts took her back to the cemetery. For a moment there, she could've sworn Jack had intended to kiss her. The magnetic attraction she'd assumed was dead had risen again, pulling her toward him. She had found herself reciting the same mantra she had in her youth: *Kiss me, Jack. Kiss me.*

But, she reminded herself, he hadn't. Maybe it had been a figment of her imagination. She'd stared into the eyes of the man she had once loved so intensely and gotten confused. But she wasn't confused about the ache in her heart. She missed him.

Brett was the last to speak, and after he was finished with his carefully scripted pitch, they all looked at Jack.

Through most of the presentation Jack had been quiet,

every now and then asking a question. Katie thought the reporters had handled them all deftly.

"Okay," Jack said. "I guess that wraps it up. Thanks for your time."

The reporters looked at Katie for a cue on how to respond. "Thanks, everyone," she said to them.

When they left, it was close to four o'clock. As she ushered the reporters out of her office, Jack's phone rang. He glanced at the displayed number and answered it. When Katie turned back, Jack was snapping his phone shut. "Apparently I have more time than I thought," he said, sounding disappointed. "That was Greg, my pilot. Albany's closed. No flights going in or out."

Marcella popped her head in. "I think I better get going, if it's okay with you, boss."

"Fine," Katie said.

Marcella glanced at Jack. "Usually I'm here till at least eight or nine o'clock at night. I mean, we all are. We're hard workers here, yessiree. It's just that it's snowing like crazy outside and I've got to pick up my kids at day care and—"

"Have a good night, Marcella," he said.

"Right," she said, blushing. She mouthed the word *gorgeous* over Jack's head.

Katie motioned for her to shut the door. She took a deep breath and said, "So…can we be honest?"

"Honest?" Jack leaned forward. He was so close, his thigh was brushing against hers.

She nodded. "Do we get the money?"

Jack's expression hardened. "I want to, but…" His voice trailed off.

"But what?"

He leaned forward and met her gaze directly. Fire blazed in his eyes as he said, "Give me a reason, Katie."

"I've spent the past two days giving you reasons."

"No," Jack said. "You've told me nothing except sentiment. I want to know why, as an objective investor, I should give you money.''

So she told him. She pulled out spreadsheets, old newspapers, new layouts and a list of awards the paper had received. When she was finished, it was close to eight o'clock and Jack was sitting in his chair with his arms crossed, a soft smile on his lips.

''What?'' she asked.

''You,'' he said. ''You've turned into quite the business-woman. Not that I'm surprised.''

''And you've turned into quite a patronizing—'' She bit her tongue, wincing. Damn! Why did she always just speak her mind like that? Jack wasn't her friend any longer; he was a business associate. She opened her eyes, expecting retribution. But he was still smiling.

''Still saying whatever pops into your head?'' he asked.

''Seems like.'' She gave an embarrassed shrug.

He stopped smiling and stood up. ''I'm going to do my best to help you, Katie.''

She nodded, not trusting herself to speak.

''Come on,'' he said. ''I'll drive you home. Even you can't ride a bike in a foot of snow.''

They put on their coats and walked to the door in silence. Katie suspected that if it was up to him alone, he would invest the money. But it wasn't. She knew he had to convince his board, and that wouldn't be easy.

But she did know one thing for a fact. He was willing to try.

Jack opened the door for her. As she stepped outside, she hit a patch of ice and slipped backward. He grabbed her waist, pulling her into him, and she felt a rush of sexual energy as she fell against him.

With his strong arms still around her, he said, ''Still not much of a skater?''

She straightened herself, breaking away from him. She

knew Jack was teasing her. A former competitive skater, she had taught *him* how to skate. "I'll take you on any day."

He laughed and together they searched the parking lot for his car. All of the cars were covered in snow, making them unrecognizable. Adding to their confusion, Jack couldn't exactly remember where or *what* he had parked. After following the sound of the remote, they scraped off a black Ford Taurus and jumped inside.

She hadn't realized just how bad the roads were until they left town. Route 23, the two-lane highway that led to her house, hadn't been plowed recently. She knew her half-mile driveway was going to be even trickier.

The snow was blowing so badly, Jack almost missed the turn. "It's right here!" she said, too late.

Jack turned the wheel but the car spun across her driveway and plowed into a ditch.

"Are you all right?" Jack asked. He had unbuckled his seat belt and was leaning over her.

One gloved hand cupped her face as the other smoothed the hair away from her eyes. The smell of leather mixed with his cologne. Feeling the stirring of passion deep inside her, she swallowed it back down. "I'm fine," she said, brushing his hands away. "Fine."

Had he noticed the effect he was having on her? Had he sensed that she was still attracted to him?

She heard him breathe a sigh of relief as he leaned back into his seat.

"I'm sorry," he said. "I just…I'm not used to driving."

"Don't tell me you have a chauffeur?" Her voice was loud, almost accusatory. She knew why. She was compensating for her true feelings, trying to make it seem as if he meant nothing to her. Nothing. He was an old friend whom she barely remembered.

"I live in the city," he said defensively. "We take cabs. Honest to God, Devonworth, do you ever keep your mouth shut?"

She shrugged.

"Climb over," he said, motioning toward his lap.

"What?" She stopped breathing again. Was this a come-on? *Right here, right now, Devonworth.*

"Climb over. I'm getting out to push. When I say go, put the car in reverse."

Jack got out of the car and shut the door. So, Katie thought, it had not been a come-on at all. Why was her mind constantly in the gutter? What was it about Jack that made her so...so sex-crazed?

She crawled into the empty driver's seat, peering through the windshield wipers at Jack. She couldn't help but smile. There was something very funny about Jack standing in a foot of snow wearing an expensive cashmere coat and Gucci loafers.

When he told her to start the car, she threw it into reverse and hit the accelerator. A wave of snow flew at Jack, but the car stayed still.

Jack started motioning frantically and she took her foot off the accelerator. Her smile turned into full-fledged laughter as she saw him covered with snow from head to toe. He walked over to the car and opened the door. "What's so funny?" he asked.

"You look like the Abominable Snowman."

"Really?" His smile faded and for a split second she was worried she had insulted him.

Something about the way she was looking at him sent him back in time. It was as if he was a kid again, hanging out with the girl he loved. His only true friend in the world. And something about the way she was sitting there laughing tempted him to pick her up and dump her in a snowbank himself, just as he would've done back then. But he stopped himself. They weren't kids anymore. And this wasn't a social visit.

He reached in front of her, turned off the car and took the key out of the ignition. "Suddenly I feel like walking," he said.

"Funny," she said, climbing out. "I was thinking the same thing."

He opened the back door and grabbed his briefcase. "Shall we?"

Snow was falling in big, fat flakes all around them. It didn't look like it would ever let up. They trudged along, cutting a path through the heavy powder. They did their best to make normal conversation, but they were too tentative and careful. Finally, Katie burst in front of him, practically dancing. "Guess who has six children. Guess!"

Jack smiled. "You got me. Who?"

"Christina Spagle. Your old girlfriend."

"She wasn't my girlfriend."

"You asked her to the junior prom."

Only, he felt like saying, because you had decided to go with Tom Klarner, the captain of the football team. Jack had not been the only boy in love with Katie Devonworth. Every single boy in school had fallen victim to her charms at one time or another. "Six kids," he said, pretending interest. "Wow."

"Just think," she said. "If you had married her—"

"I would never have married her."

"Well, if you had, you'd be sitting at home right now, with Jack Jr. and little Jackie and Jacqueline…"

"I've named all my kids after me?"

"Sure. Why not?" She smiled. "George Foreman did."

"He did?"

"Yup. George Jr. George the third. Frieda George…"

"So I could've had a Frieda Jack?"

"Sure."

"Unfortunately, even that wouldn't have been enough to make me marry Christina."

"Oh, yeah? Why not?" Katie was standing in front of him now. *Because I loved you,* he felt like shouting. The snow had once again fallen on her long, lush lashes. Her hands were on her slim hips. She held her slightly pointed nose high as her lips curled into a half smile. She was daring him. But daring him to do what?

He said, "She wasn't my type."

"Well," she said as she resumed walking, "she was the type of half the guys in school."

They had reached her house and Katie bounded up the snow-covered steps, taking them two at a time. Jack grinned. He had dated a lot of women in New York, but none of them came close to Katie. Most would have waited for him to clear the snow away before they made such an attempt. That idea would never have occurred to Katie. She was her own woman, fierce and independent, and she always had been.

She pushed open the door. She hadn't bothered locking it, of course. No one in Newport Falls did. Jack was glad to see that hadn't changed.

"Come on in," she said.

Jack wasn't prepared for what he saw inside. The house was bare, stripped of its most valuable furnishings. "What happened to the furniture?" he asked, looking around.

"Oh," she said as the polite smile faded. "I sold it."

"But why?"

"I didn't have a choice."

Jack felt as if he had been punched in the stomach. He knew things had been rough at the paper, but Katie was the owner. After all, her father had always done well enough. But then again…Jack thought of Matt and their divorce. He wondered what percentage of the paper, if any, Matt had gained in the divorce.

"Oh, shoot," Katie was saying, flipping the light switch on and off. "The snow must've knocked the power out."

"Did Matt take it?"

"What?"

"Did Matt get the furniture…or a stake in the paper?"

* * *

Katie felt a sudden embarrassment as she glanced around the empty room, seeing it as if for the first time. How it had changed since Jack had last seen it! "No. The split was very amicable, just like our marriage. There was never—" She paused, looking Jack in the eye. "There was never any passion, so to speak. We were great friends in the beginning, okay friends in the end." She nodded toward the fireplace. "I better get some wood in here so we can build a fire."

"I'll get it," Jack said. "Why don't you get some candles or flashlights." He nodded toward the back. "You still have wood in the shed?"

She nodded. "I think so."

Jack gave her one last look before heading outside.

The look was enough to send shivers down her spine. It was a hungry look, the same way he had looked at her that day by the creek. Or was it? The light was dim, so perhaps she was just imagining it.

She fumbled through her kitchen drawers, searching for matches. When she found an old package, she lit the candles on the fireplace. They were red, from Christmas. She hadn't bothered to change them after the holidays.

What would happen if Jack ended up stuck here? she wondered. What would she do with him? Perhaps his pilot or valet or whatever he was would find a way to retrieve him. If not…he would spend the night. Where else would he go?

She glanced at the couch, the last piece of furniture left in the room. For a minute she saw the two of them, sitting at opposite ends, not speaking. She thought of the tense silence that would fill the room, the awkward conversation.

When a branch banged on the window, she looked at the snow swirling outside. It was beautiful, no doubt, but also a little intimidating. Mother Nature had been known to wreak havoc in Newport Falls. Snowstorms and ice storms could last days. It might be nice to have some company tonight, she thought. Not to mention some help with the fire. She doubted the power would be turned back on any time soon and it was already cold in the house, even with the furnace.

She took one of the candles with her and headed upstairs to find some warm blankets. She glanced back toward the couch. This time, instead of seeing her and Jack on opposite ends, she saw them under the blanket, huddled together. She saw Jack without a shirt, his muscular body illuminated in the moonlight. She felt his strong arms around her, felt him pull her in to him, felt him touch her breasts and—

"Cold?" Jack was standing at the foot of the stairs with a pile of wood in his arms. He nodded toward her and said, "You're shivering."

"A little." She wrapped her arms across her chest.

"I'll start the fire, but then I have to chop some more wood. This is the last of it."

"But Burt— You remember Burt Weasley, don't you? He took down a tree for me and cut up the wood—"

"Into logs. But it needs to be split." He dumped the wood beside her fireplace and opened the grate. "Where's your ax?"

"It should be in the shed. But you don't have to do it. I'll do it."

"Don't be ridiculous."

"Who do you think usually does it?" she snapped. "Besides, you're not exactly a frontiersman anymore, are you? Look at your fancy loafers," she told him. "They're ruined."

"Katie," he said, throwing some wood on the grate, "I could care less about my shoes. But if you want to chop the wood, be my guest."

"Fine." She stomped past him, grabbing her coat and heading out the door. Once outside, she stopped. Why was she so mad, anyway? He was just trying to be nice, offering to chop her wood. Why did she act as if he had just laid down an insult?

What was wrong with getting a little help? She thought of her brief marriage to Matt. He had never helped her with the household chores. Although he appreciated her paycheck, he still expected her to have all the responsibilities of a stay-at-home wife. It was her job to make dinner, clean the house and shop for groceries. When she pointed this out, he had acted defensive, almost angry. The tension between them seemed to grow worse each day. Their lovemaking, though never intense, ceased. Matt could sense her distance and it angered him. But try as she did, she couldn't make herself feel something that just wasn't there. She knew on some level he had always blamed Jack for their lack of passion. Jack was there, between them, the unspoken rift. It was enough to send Matt into the arms of another woman.

And could she blame him? As much as she cared about Matt, no man had ever excited her like Jack Reilly. She had never seen Jack without wanting to touch him, wanting him to hold her....

She made her way through the blinding snow, tripping and falling flat on her face. She picked herself up and hurried to the shed. After a couple of tries, she managed to yank open the door. She caught sight of the thick, wooden logs, tree stumps almost, that Burt had stacked on the floor. She grabbed the ax and swung it into the wood. She did it again and again, and stopped. She had barely made a dent.

She wiped back the wetness from her eyes, finally realizing she was crying. And she knew why. These were not tears of sadness, but anger. She was mad not at Jack, but at herself. Here Jack was, after all these years, and she still wanted him. She still wanted to feel his arms around her. Yet she felt paralyzed.

Matt had once accused her of being incapable of receiving or enjoying physical love. She thought she hadn't enjoyed sex with him because she wasn't attracted to him. But maybe he was right, maybe she was incapable of passion.

She picked up the ax again and held it over her head.

But Jack was there. He grabbed it from her and said,

"You've proved your point. I'll take it from here, Danielle Boone."

Katie didn't argue. She handed the ax to Jack, feeling a prickle of heat as their fingers touched.

If there was any connection, Jack was oblivious. "You're ice cold," he said. "Go back in and get warm."

But she didn't leave. She stood against the back of the building, watching as Jack chopped the wood. His muscular arms were covered by his coat, but still she could imagine the muscles working, stretching and contracting as he raised his arms over his head and slammed the blade into the wood.

She thought back to the cemetery. She had felt so close to him there. Now she imagined running her fingers through his thick hair. Feeling his lips against hers. Feeling his hands against her back, pulling her into him.

Jack stopped and turned back toward her. "You're still here?"

She had one night. One night and then Jack would leave her again. He would because he had to. He couldn't stay here in Newport Falls. He didn't love her, never had. Still, it was obvious he cared. But was it enough to make love to her? Would he give her one night of passion? One night that she could remember for the rest of her life?

And could she do that? Could she sleep with him, knowing that he would leave her once again? That her heart was guaranteed pain?

But maybe, she thought, this time would be different. No longer was Jack the insecure kid, and no longer was she the rich newspaperman's daughter.

Now Jack was a man of the world. He had dated some of the most beautiful and desirable women in the country. But then why, she thought, would he want her? He could have any woman he wanted.

"Katie?" he said, still waiting for an answer.

Looking into his eyes, she could feel her heart melt. This was Jack, *her* Jack. And damned if she didn't love him as much as ever.

"I better go start dinner," she whispered.

Five

Katie finished cracking the eggs into the pan just as the door blew open.

Jack barely looked at her as he marched past her. She could hear him dump the wood beside the fireplace. He said, "I think it's snowed another foot since we got back. Does it ever stop snowing here?"

"No," she joked. "Never."

He walked back into the kitchen.

"I've laid out some dry clothes for you," she said. "And I've set some boots out, as well."

He crossed his arms. "You just happen to have men's things lying around?"

"They're Matt's. I keep finding stuff that belongs to him. I just haven't had a chance to get rid of it all."

He leaned in the doorway. "You haven't seen him for a while?"

"No. He left a couple of years ago. Rather suddenly and not alone."

"What do you mean?"

"I mean, Matt was having an affair."

"What?" Jack's tone conveyed his disbelief.

Katie nodded.

"I—I can't believe it," he said.

At the time, she couldn't, either. Sweet, sensitive Matt. It was only afterward that it all sank in. How hurt he must have been to turn to someone else.

Jack shook his head. "That son of a bitch."

"It wasn't all his fault."

"What?"

"There was more to it than that. I wasn't the best wife in the world."

Jack swallowed. "You were…unfaithful?"

"Me?" she laughed. "Hardly. But I don't think I ever cared about Matt the way he wanted me to."

"Why not?" Jack asked.

She looked at him. He had no clue as to the role he had played in their breakup. She shook her head and stirred the eggs again. "It was just one of those things, I guess."

Jack nodded. He turned to leave the room, and a moment later she heard him talking on his phone. She pulled out a couple of her mother's china plates and headed back toward the living-room fire. When she saw Jack she stopped. He stood there in Matt's jeans, without a shirt.

She was right. His muscular physique hadn't changed at all since high school. He still looked like a natural-born body-builder. Unable to avert her eyes, she watched as he pulled a T-shirt down over his flat stomach. The T-shirt was a size too small. And it was no wonder. Matt, although physically fit, was no competition for Jack. He never had been.

He glanced at the plates and said, "Good idea. It's much warmer in here than in the kitchen. Whatever you're making in there smells great."

"Just eggs," she said. "I'm afraid I haven't gone grocery

shopping for a while." She set the plates in front of the fire. "Did I hear you talking on the phone?"

"Yes," he said, pulling on some socks. "Greg called from the airport. He wanted to know if he should rent a truck or something and come plow me out."

She stopped. "And what did you say?"

He was watching her carefully. "I said it wouldn't do much good, unless he could attach wings to it and make it fly."

"So, you're staying tonight." It was more a statement than a question. She went back into the kitchen to grab some silverware.

"If that's okay," he said, following her.

"Sure," she said. "We can...catch up."

"Exactly," he said.

She turned and looked at him, waiting. But waiting for what? "Of course," she said, "if you want to use my phone to call anyone, you know, to reschedule..." Like Carol, she thought. She picked up the old green rotary phone attached to the wall. There wasn't any dial tone. "Or not."

"I don't need your phone, anyway," he said. He took the phone out of her hands and put it back on the receiver. "I have one, remember? I just hung up."

"I just thought you might want to call Carol," she managed to say as nonchalantly as possible.

"Carol?" he asked. "My assistant will deal with her."

"Oh," she said. Of course. Why bother canceling a date himself? No. He'd rather have his assistant do the dirty work for him.

"I'll do that," he said, taking the silverware from her hands.

Suddenly, she smelled something burning. The eggs! She grabbed the spatula, but they were ruined, burned to a crisp.

"They're fine," Jack said over her shoulder.

She picked up the pan and dumped them in the garbage. "You're just being nice."

She set the pan back on the stove and cracked another egg.

"Why don't I make dinner?" Jack offered.

"That's okay."

"You're still in your wet clothes," he said. "Go change."

"Are you sure?" she asked.

"Positive. I've done this before." He grinned. Suddenly he transformed from a ruthless mogul into a sweetheart.

Grateful, she smiled. Handing Jack the pan, she grabbed a candle and headed upstairs.

She searched through her drawers, looking for something suitable to wear. Something that looked good, but didn't imply she was *trying* to look good.

Ugh! When would she stop trying to impress Jack? It made no difference to him whether she wore a black negligee or a potato sack.

She thought back to some of the women he had dated. The ones whose photographs had appeared over the AP wire. Beautiful and brilliant, rich…

How could she ever hope to compete? It was a waste of energy to try. She would only end up making a fool of herself. She pulled out her old purple sweats and put them on.

By the time she got back downstairs, Jack had dinner ready. He had put a candle on the floor in front of the fireplace and a place setting on either side.

The eggs were prepared perfectly, and before she knew it she had finished them. Once again, Jack was looking at her with a bemused smile. "Do you want me to make you some more?" he asked.

"No," she said, embarrassed she had eaten so much. "But they were really good. Do you still like to cook?"

"I never cook anymore," he said.

"I remember," she said, "when you used to love it."

He smiled and said, "I did it because I had to. And I never made anything more than hot dogs and eggs."

"I know. But they were good."

"Now, your mother," he said, "was a good cook."

Her mother had loved to try new recipes. Except for special

occasions, which were always celebrated in the dining room of the inn downtown, her mother had made dinner and dessert almost every night of her life. Jack had attended many of her mother's homemade dinners.

He continued, "But I take it you didn't inherit a knack for the kitchen."

She laughed. "Hardly." She glanced around the house. "It's been hard around here without her."

"I know," Jack said. "I'm sorry."

Katie looked at him and said, "Why *didn't* you call when she died?"

Jack glanced down. "I thought you wouldn't notice that I didn't call."

"Not notice? Jack! You were one of my best friends."

"But we hadn't talked in years."

"But I still cared about you. I still thought about you and wondered how you were doing."

"I'm sorry. I thought Matt would take care of you."

"Matt has nothing to do with this. You and I were friends, independent of Matt." She put down her fork. "Besides, I wasn't in need of someone to take care of me. But I could've used a friend. I went through a hard time. My father, and my mother dying, then Matt leaving…not to mention what was going on around me. The struggle to keep the newspaper afloat when every day I heard that some other place was closing, some other family was leaving town…" Her voice faded. "Listen to me complain. Sorry. It doesn't usually get to me like this."

He touched her hand and he ran his fingers lightly over her knuckles, causing her heart to beat faster. "I'm sorry," he said.

She forced herself to pull her hand away, then, grabbing the plates, headed back into the kitchen, where she set them in the sink.

Jack followed her into the kitchen. "We'll wash them later," he said.

He was standing directly behind her. She could feel him, sense his masculine presence. Her sudden desire was strong enough to make her tremble.

Jack put his hands on her arms. "You're shivering again," he said. "Let's get you by the fire."

She didn't resist as Jack led her back into the living room and sat her down on the couch. He tossed another log into the fire. He turned back toward her and said, "So, because I didn't call you when your mom died...that's why you didn't come to me before? That's why you didn't tell me how bad things were around here?"

She stared into the fire. "I thought you knew."

"How would I know? The only people I was close to were you and Matt."

"I guess I didn't think you'd care."

It was completely dark outside. The only light came from the candles and fire.

"Let's face it," she continued, "it's common knowledge that you couldn't wait to leave this place. That you couldn't wait to leave me."

Jack sat down next to her. He was stunned. This was what she'd thought—that he didn't care about her? All those years he spent pining for her, the devastation he felt when she married Matt... She had no knowledge of anything?

She said, "Was I wrong?"

He looked at her. Her brown eyes had welled with tears. The bravado was gone. Now she was just Katie. Sweet, vulnerable Katie.

"I always cared about you," he said. "I still do."

They sat there, side by side, neither speaking. It was not an awkward silence, like they had endured previously. It was the quiet that comes with being old friends, when words weren't necessary.

After a while, Katie closed her eyes. Jack knew she was exhausted. He knew how hard she had been working, the weight of the challenge she had taken on. Did she ever have fun anymore? He doubted it.

He thought of his old friend, Matt. How dare he hurt her like that! Though he'd been lucky enough to marry her, he hadn't appreciated her. But Katie acted as if she was to blame for Matt's infidelities. Good-hearted Katie, who refused to see the bad in her friends. Or the weakness.

Jack was surprised there was no sign at all that Matt had even lived there. Besides the lack of furniture, everything was just as Jack remembered it. The walls were still covered with the same family photos that had been there for years. A portrait of Katie's grandfather, the one who had started the newspaper. A picture of her father in front of the paper's office. A wedding picture of her parents.

One thing had changed, however. The house and property that had once stood so proud and beautiful had fallen into disrepair. The shed that her father had built with his own hands was ready to be condemned. The house itself was not much better, with cracked and water-stained ceilings, peeling wallpaper, threadbare carpets. Yet, he had to admit, the house retained the warmth and love of the Devonworth family. He was envious of Katie, envious that she had a place she cared enough about to fight for. A house that was truly a home.

He thought of his apartment in the city. It was grand and sleek, full of the best his designer could find. Expensive artwork, gleaming hardwood floors, faux-finished walls. But he would've traded his place in a split second for a home like this.

Still, he couldn't envy Katie's situation. He had been saddened to see the upstairs as empty as the downstairs. Even her bedroom contained only an old four-poster bed and a small chest of drawers. As he thought about her predicament he felt another stab of pain and regret. If only Katie had come to him earlier, before she sold all of her furnishings, he could've given her money, could've helped her salvage her business before it was too late.

Katie rested her head on Jack's shoulder, and he pulled her closer, feeling the quiet ache of his muscles tightening. They were still rubbery from chopping wood. His daily gym workouts couldn't compare with getting exercise the natural way. He never thought there would come a day when he missed chopping wood, but apparently he'd guessed wrong. Just as he had about a lot of things. Like Katie. He'd dated more than his share of women, but she was still the most stubborn, opinionated and unbelievably sexy woman he had ever encountered.

He thought of Alexa, his most recent conquest. She was beautiful, sweet, eager to please. Everything a man could desire. Still, he had broken up with her. His friends had thought him crazy. You'll never find another like her, they'd said. But he didn't want one like her. He wanted Katie.

As he listened to Katie's soft, even breath and felt the weight of her body leaning against him, he thought again of that moment at the creek. He'd spent so much time rehashing the past, but he couldn't stop thinking how different life might have been if only he'd possessed the courage to tell Katie how he felt that day. Or anytime thereafter. But he hadn't. Nor had he been there for her when she needed him. He'd disappointed the only person who had ever really meant anything to him.

Many times Katie had helped him out of bad situations. On many of those occasions, he'd been tempted to tell her how he really felt about her. One time in particular stood out in his mind. About six months before that fateful day at the creek, he had gotten in a fight with his father. It was a bad fight, a physical one. Afterward, he had been so upset that he had gone to the Devonworth house. Since it was nearly midnight and he knew everyone would be asleep, he had climbed up the old willow tree to the roof, slid down toward Katie's bedroom and tapped lightly on her window. A few seconds later, she opened the window.

"What are you doing here?" Katie had asked.

"I got in a fight with my dad." In fact, his father had broken a beer bottle and tried to cut him. Jack had ducked out of the way, but not fast enough. The jagged edge of the bottle had caught him above the eye.

Katie grabbed his hand and helped him inside. She shut the window against the November chill and turned to face him. Her long brown hair was backlit by the moon, making her look like a beautiful angel. Her white flannel gown was sheer enough for him to make out the gentle curves of her breasts, and her full, round hips.

Her eyes widened as she saw the ugly red gash above his eye. "You're hurt."

She went to touch it and he grabbed her hand. "It's nothing," he said.

"Oh, Jack," she whispered, and she looked as if she might cry. "Your father did this, didn't he?"

Jack hung his head, embarrassed.

"I'll get a washcloth for you," Katie said quickly.

He sat on the edge of her bed, for a moment regretting coming there. What was he thinking, showing up in the middle of the night and dragging her into his private hell?

She came back with a cool cloth and held it to his eye. This time he didn't stop her. The cloth felt good, but her comfort felt incredible. "I'm sorry I bothered you," he said. "I didn't know where else to go."

"You did the right thing." She slipped her other arm around him and hugged him as she held his head.

She knew better than to ask for details. This type of thing had happened many times before. There was nothing anyone could do.

The next morning, they woke up in each other's arms. Jack heard her father walk down the hall and pause outside her room. "Katie?" he called out. "Time to wake up."

Startled, Katie motioned for Jack to hide in the closet. He did, shutting himself in just as her father opened the door.

"What time is it?" Katie asked her father sweetly. She was always asking the time.

"Nearly eight."

"I better hurry," she said. "Jack's coming over for breakfast this morning. He's supposed to be here at eight."

"Well, then," her father said, "you have exactly four minutes." Once he shut her door, Katie walked over to the closet and opened it. She was smiling from ear to ear. "I'll meet you downstairs."

In the daylight, Katie's gown provided no more coverage than a sheer shift. She stood in front of him with one arm on her hip, unaware of her staggering beauty. Jack was overcome by the urge to take Katie into his arms and make love to her. The intensity of his lust was so strong, so overpowering that he found it difficult to speak.

"Well?" she said. "Aren't you hungry?"

"Starving," he managed to say, before stepping around her and climbing out the window. He never went to her bedroom in the middle of the night again.

That memory had haunted his dreams for years. He could see Katie in her gown, feel the guilt for not being able to look away. But he still couldn't. After all this time, he would've given his right arm to make love to her right there on her childhood bed.

Now, after all these years, he was going to be sleeping in her house again. The thought of spending the night with her was enough to make him sweat. It had been a while since he'd been with a woman, and he was hungry. Had he been back in New York, there would have been a number of women he could call, any of whom would have been more than happy to share his bed. But he knew he was kidding himself. Even if he was back in New York, he wouldn't call these women. There was only one woman he wanted to make love to tonight, and that was Katie Devonworth.

As he looked down at her beautiful face, he grew stiff with desire. Not tonight, he warned himself. He needed to take things slow, to win back her trust. He needed to prove to her that he was the man she was meant to be with.

As gently as he could, he slid out from underneath Katie, setting her head on the pillow. He covered her with the blankets. Then he grabbed an old pillow and stretched out on the floor.

But it was a long time before he fell asleep.

Six

Katie opened her eyes. Morning light flooded the room. With a start she sat up straight. What time was it? And where was Jack?

Wherever he was, he had tended to the fire. It was blazing, the freshly cut wood crackling.

"Jack?" she called. She stood and walked toward the stairs, wrapping the blanket around her. The living room was cozy and warm, but the rest of the house was still freezing. "Jack?"

She heard the back door slam and saw Jack walk in carrying a bundle of wood. He was wearing his cashmere coat and the boots she had set out for him the night before. With messy hair and a day's worth of a dark beard he looked even more handsome than before. Dangerously sexy, she thought, the same look he had when they were kids.

"Good morning," he said, walking past her.

"Good morning," she replied, stepping out of his way. She

watched him stack the wood next to the fireplace. "I see it's still snowing."

"With no sign of stopping," he said.

"I take it the power is still off."

"As well as the phone."

"You tried to call someone?" she asked. Her voice sounded shrill and accusatory. Right away, she tried to make amends. "Not that you're not welcome, because of course you are…."

"I was using my computer. I tried to go online."

"What time is it?"

"A little before nine."

She glanced around, suddenly needing a cup of coffee. Badly. "I think I have some instant coffee somewhere," she said. "We can boil some water."

"No thanks," he said. "I don't drink coffee."

"Tea?"

"Nor tea. But I'd be happy to make you some."

"That's all right," she began.

He put his hand on her shoulder. "I have the feeling you're not waited on much. Let me do it."

She hesitated. "Okay," she said. "Coffee, please."

As he left the room, she tugged the blanket up to her shoulders, grateful for the warmth from the fire. She glanced at the pillow on the floor. The corporate Don Juan had been a perfect gentleman.

Jack walked back in. "How did you sleep?"

"Good," she said. "Surprisingly."

"Why surprisingly?"

"I mean, considering you were here with me. It's been a long time since I've slept with anyone."

"Oh?"

"Ah, well," Katie said, blushing, "you know what I mean."

"Have you dated much since you and Matt broke up?" he asked, as casually as if he was mentioning the weather.

"I've been on exactly two dates since Matt. One was with a dentist from Granville. The other was with the cousin of a man who worked for me. He sells tires in Albany. Both dates were miserable and neither was repeated."

"Something wrong with the men?"

"No. They were fine. I just…I wasn't interested in dating."

"So why'd you go?"

"Because I'm thirty-two years old. If I'm not careful, one of these days I'm going to end up all by myself with a big old dirty house and a bunch of cats."

He laughed. "I doubt that."

She watched him at the fire as he opened the kettle and stirred the icy water. "What about you?" she asked. "Certainly one of those lovely women you've squired about would concede to marry you."

He laughed. "I don't think so."

"Of course they would. You're a catch. Never been married. Rich, handsome, funny—" She stopped, embarrassed.

"That's okay. I won't tell anyone you referred to me as handsome or funny."

He took the water off the fire and poured it into a cup. He mixed in some coffee crystals and handed it to her. "It must get lonely, living in this big house all by yourself." He was sitting down next to her, so close their legs were touching.

She took a sip of her coffee. "Sometimes," she said. "But I'm hardly ever here."

A strand of hair fell over her eyes. Jack caught it and tucked it behind her ear. "So," he said quietly, "what do you do for fun?"

He didn't remove his hand. He was still touching the side of her face, his fingers gently circling her cheek.

"Fun?"

"How do you relax?"

Her heart was in her throat, and she was having a difficult time focusing on anything but the feel of his fingers.

"What's the matter, Katie?" he asked softly.

She swallowed and closed her eyes. His fingers were trailing down now, underneath the neck of her sweatshirt. Just enough to tease, to torment. "What are you doing?" she whispered.

"Does this feel good?" he asked quietly.

"Y-yes," she managed to say.

"I might be able to help you...relax," he said.

Katie closed her eyes as his other hand crept inside her shirt. His fingers touched her lightly, making their way toward her breasts. This was her big chance. What she had been waiting for. They could make love straight through until they were plowed out. They could make love...until Jack left. He would return to his life in New York and she would stay here, with only a memory for company. But she was not as strong as she had been in high school. His rejection, especially if she gave him her body, as well as her heart, would cut much worse.

Katie's eyes snapped open. She forced herself to stand. "It's hard to relax when I'm so worried about the paper. When I'm so worried about my community," she said. "I'm not like you. I've never been one to walk away from my commitments."

It was as if she had doused him with a bucket of cold water. Jack stiffened and pulled away. As she looked at his furrowed brow, she could tell her remark had hit its target. She glanced toward the window. "Maybe we should see if we can get your car out."

"Great idea," he said abruptly.

"I'll help you. Just give me a minute to get dressed."

"No, that's all right," he said, walking past her.

"Wait." She stopped him at the door. "So, if you do get your car out..." She hesitated. Are you going to leave just like this? she wanted to ask. Will you just drive away? Will I ever hear from you again?

She looked into his steely blue eyes. He met her gaze and said, "If I get my car out, then I doubt I'll make it back up your driveway. I'm going to head directly to the airport. I'll have these boots sent back to you, if that's all right."

In other words, yes, he would disappear from her life once again.

"There's no rush." Her voice masked the emotions she felt.

"Thanks for everything. I'll have someone call you on Monday with a decision." He grabbed his computer and paused. "Goodbye, Katie." He held out the same hand that had caressed her so tenderly only moments before. Katie grasped it and he gave her a quick, impersonal shake. And with that, he was gone.

Jack practically charged out of the house. What had he been thinking, making a pass? It was too soon, dammit! Much too soon. But he just couldn't seem to help himself. It wasn't enough to be near her. He needed to be touching her, to be kissing her. He wanted to take her in his arms and make love to her.

And there were moments, moments when she looked at him, that he could swear she felt the same way. Yet every time he made an attempt she shot him down.

It was going to take time, Jack realized. Lots of time before she would trust him again.

Jack approached his car, buried under a mound of snow. Getting it out wasn't going to be easy, but he had little choice. He needed to get back to New York and prove to Katie that he cared about her. He wasn't sure what he could do to save the *The Falls*, which she loved so much, but he knew one thing. He had to try.

If the board of directors wouldn't free up the money, he would use his own cash. But, he reminded himself, that wouldn't be easy. Almost everything was tied up in his London deal. There wasn't much liquid. No, he thought. There was no easy way to get Katie the kind of money she needed.

A foot of snow had fallen since the car had slipped off the

driveway, covering the tire tracks and footprints from the night before. He glanced toward the road, which hadn't been cleared, then looked up at the cloudy, snow-filled sky. It was obvious that without a miracle he would be stuck here another day.

With all his strength he managed to open the car door, then put his computer inside. He kicked at the snow behind the car, trying to make a path. He was just beginning to curse himself for not having thought to bring a shovel when he heard "You might try a shovel."

He turned around to see Katie standing behind him. She was wearing black ski pants that clung to her like a second skin, and a big orange parka and a brightly colored stocking cap. In her mittened hands she held two shovels.

She shook her head as she handed him one. "City boy, city boy," she murmured, loud enough for him to hear.

He took the shovel and said, "What are you doing?"

"One, I need a ride into the office, and two, I took pity on you. I couldn't stand the thought of you tunneling out with your hands. But even with shovels, we've got our work cut out for us."

Jack didn't answer; instead he focused his energy on digging out his car. After a while, he said, "How about you drive again and I'll push."

"Okay." Her tone of voice let him know she thought he was crazy.

Katie started up the car and Jack pushed, barking out orders to alternate gears. After a while, Katie turned off the car and leaned out the window. "I've got some bad news," she said. "You're not going anywhere. Not by car, at least."

Jack leaned against the car. "I'm coming to the same conclusion myself."

"I hope you're not missing anything important today," she said.

Jack shook his head. "Some meetings. That's all."

"With Carol?" she asked.

He stopped, surprised that she was once again mentioning Carol, his senior strategist, a fancy term for one hell of a good accountant. She was the one responsible for coming up with the money for his deals. But of course Katie would know who she was. He was certain she had done research on his company before she had invited him out to lunch.

"Among others," he said, catching her eye.

"Others?" She stepped out of the car and slammed the door. Her tone was icy as she handed him his computer. "Well, I'm sure they'll all be terribly disappointed." And with that, she stomped off toward the street.

"Katie?" he said. "Where are you going?"

"Where do you think? To work!"

"You're going to walk five miles through a blizzard?"

She motioned around her. "This…snow is hardly a blizzard. Maybe it's just too much for a city boy like you, but—"

"City boy or country girl. It's too much for any human."

She stopped walking and spun around to face him. "I have to get to work. Everyone is depending on me."

"That's not the reason and you know it."

"Know what?"

"You'd rather walk miles in a blizzard than spend another minute with me. You're afraid of me. Afraid of what might happen if we spend another night together."

Katie raised her eyebrows, a grin crossing her lips. "You certainly think highly of yourself."

"Not really," he said. "I just know what I'm feeling. There's still something between us, Katie. Maybe we should figure out what the hell it is."

The grin was gone. "I know what it is. It's like you've completely forgotten the past. You're treating me like I'm a stranger, like I'm auditioning to be one of your women. You're here with me and you think, what the heck? Why not? Might as well."

"Might as well what?"

"You know what. And as much as I'm tempted—believe me, I'm tempted—I can't."

She plopped down on the back of the car, her arms crossed against her chest.

He sat next to her. "Why not?"

"There are a million reasons, but mostly because I know you. I think it's pretty clear we're not right for each other."

"Oh?"

"Look, I need a different type of guy."

She couldn't have inflicted more pain if she'd slapped him. "I know lots of guys," he joked, trying to mask his hurt feelings. "What type are you looking for?"

"Someone I can give my heart to. Someone I can trust."

"Matt really hurt you, didn't he?" His anger was so intense, the name burned his mouth as he said it.

"Matt? He hurt me. But probably not as much as he wished."

Jack was silent for a moment. "Do you think you'll ever trust a man again?"

"I hope so."

"But you don't even allow yourself to date."

"If it's meant to be, it will happen. I haven't thrown in the towel yet. But I want it to be special this time. Romantic."

"Wasn't it special with Matt?"

She shrugged.

"But…you married him."

"My mom was dying."

"That's why you married him?" he asked. He swallowed, waiting for the answer.

After what seemed like an eternity, she sighed. Her eyes met his. "Had I been feeling better about myself and my life, we never would've gotten together."

Remorse washed over him. It was his fault, all of it. Had he been there for Katie, had he been physically with her, she would not have married Matt. Instead he had abandoned her when she needed him most.

"Matt and I, well, we never really had that romantic kind of love. It was always rather awkward and forced."

Jack was no longer breathing. He couldn't stand to hear about her relationship with Matt, but he forced himself to listen. It was his penance, the least he could do. "I'm sorry," he heard himself say.

"I always thought I'd marry the man who swept me away, who made me see fireworks or something. But it didn't happen that way."

Life had not been kind to Katie. Yet he, her best friend, had been too hurt to provide any comfort. Jack felt the urge to put his arms around her and promise to never let go. Instead, he nudged her arm and said, "Hey."

"What?"

"You're wearing my hat." It had just caught his attention. She was wearing a knit cap with a long tail and pom-pom on the end. As a kid she was always losing her scarf and complaining about a cold neck, so one year he had bought her that hat. "You'll never be cold again," he had told her when he gave her the hat and wrapped the tail around her neck.

And, after all those years, it was still keeping her neck warm. "This hat?" she asked.

"I gave it to you for Christmas, junior year."

She was starting to smile. "So what are you saying? Do you want it back?"

"No. I was just making a point. You know, that maybe you were right about being stuck here with me and all, but I'm not exactly a stranger, am I?"

"I misspoke," she said. "I meant pain in the ass."

She had started walking again, faster this time. *"Devonworth,"* he growled. "You better watch out. Those are fighting words."

She laughed. "Oh, really, *Reilly?* Coming from the man who tried to tunnel his way out of a snowdrift with his hands. The man who's wearing no hat, just a million-dollar coat and carrying a million-dollar computer. Just what do you think you're going to do to—"

She didn't have time to finish. Because Jack had already set his computer in the car and was running in her direction. She dropped her shovel and took off back toward the house. But she was no match for Jack. He grabbed her by the waist and hoisted her off the ground. "Put me down," she yelled.

"I'm afraid I can't do that."

"Why not?"

Still holding her around the waist, he made his way toward a giant snowbank.

"Because I'm a pain in the ass, remember?" He held her up on top of the snowbank.

She was laughing in spite of herself, kicking her legs.

"Kick all you want. You're going in."

"All right, I'm sorry. I'm sorry I called you a pain in the ass."

He turned her around so that her face was only inches from his. Her beauty was so overwhelming it took his breath away. Her brown eyes were big and bright. The cold made her cheeks glow and her lips look ripe and luscious. He could feel his manhood rise to attention and press against his pants.

She continued, "I meant to say, pain in the *rear.*"

"You've left me no choice," he said, and dropped her in the snow. He turned around and began walking back toward the house.

"Oh, Jack!" she said. And then he felt it, a ball of snow right at the back of his head. And then he felt another and another. Katie Devonworth was still the best damn snowball thrower in the county.

He ran around the side of the garage and prepared his own ammunition. He stuffed snowballs in his pockets in between returning missiles. After a while, he walked out from behind the garage. "All right," he said. "Enough."

She stood up from behind the snowbank. "Getting cold,

city boy? Or just tired of getting pummeled by a girl?'' she asked, with a teasing tone.

He held his hands in the air, surrendering. ''I give up. I'm ready to concede that we're strangers.''

''You're unarmed?''

He nodded. ''Yep,'' he said, still walking toward her.

''That wasn't very smart, was it?'' she said as a snowball whizzed past his ear.

He pulled out the hastily made balls of snow and went running toward her. She yelled and popped down behind the snowbank, but he jumped over it, landing next to her. Before she could grab another snowball, he was on her. He straddled her on the ground, holding her arms.

Her hat had fallen off and her long brown hair was splayed across the snow. Katie Devonworth was still the most beautiful woman he had ever seen in his life. He had to tell her how he felt about her. How much he still thought of her. How much he still cared. ''Katie,'' he began. But he couldn't speak. He didn't want to talk. He wanted to kiss her.

Despite the chill around him, warmth flowed through his limbs and into his engorged self. His desire was now a need that begged satisfaction. He bent over her, his eyes focused on her lips. Just one kiss, he promised himself. One kiss and he would be satisfied....

But he knew better than that. Katie had made it clear where she stood on the subject of old friends making love in the middle of a blizzard. Using every ounce of willpower and strength he possessed, he jumped off and helped her up. ''It's been a long time since I had fun like this,'' he said.

''I know that's not true,'' she said. ''I've seen pictures of you with all of your women. You seem to be having plenty of fun to me.''

''All of my women?''

''You know, society belles and what have you. Sometimes the AP runs photos of you over the wire.''

Jack shrugged. It embarrassed him to think that Katie had

seen any of the women he had been with. He wanted to tell her that none of them meant anything to him. That no other woman compared to her. Instead he said, "I date."

"But?"

"No buts. It doesn't necessarily mean I'm having fun."

"Too much fun to marry one," she said sarcastically.

She started to walk back to the house and he hurried to catch up. He said, "I haven't gotten married because…well, none of them has been right for me."

She rolled her eyes. "You're one of those."

"One of what?"

"Those men who hold out hope that the perfect woman really does exist."

"I don't hold out hope," he said, looking directly at Katie. "I know."

But Katie didn't get it. "What time is it?"

Jack smiled as he checked his watch. "Almost noon."

She motioned for him to follow her. "Let's go make lunch. I'm thinking bread and cheese."

"That sounds great," he said. "Thanks."

"Okay," she said, noticing the lock of hair that fell over his eyes. Jack had always had thick, beautiful hair with a mind of its own. These days he may wear designer clothes, but his hair still had the same cowlicks. "Sure." Bread and eggs it was. Or was that bread and cheese? Whatever it was, she never ate it. Nor did she prepare it. Because as soon as she got back inside, her cell phone rang. It was Kurt, her assistant editor. He had braved the weather and made it in to work, along with a handful of other dedicated souls. Together they had a paper to get out. She planted herself in front of the fire and began to give directives.

Hours later, she had finished up one paper and gotten a solid start on the next. Production of *The Falls* would not be interrupted by the storm.

She leaned forward on the couch and massaged her aching

shoulders. Her head was pounding and her throat hurt from talking.

"Rough day at the office?" Jack said. He handed her a steaming cup.

"What is it?" she asked.

"It's tea."

She smiled, touched by his kindness. "How did you make it?"

"I boiled some water in the fire. Right in front of you. You were so busy you didn't notice."

The aroma of her cinnamon tea filled the room. She breathed in the steamy scent and tasted the warm liquid. She could feel herself begin to relax. "Thank you," she said. "It's delicious."

"Are you done for the day?"

"For better or worse. I'm not sure what kind of paper we put together, but it's going out."

"I admire your fortitude."

"Is that what it's called?" she said, smiling.

Jack pushed a plate with bread and cheese in her direction. "You have to be hungry."

Jack had done his best to make it look appetizing, arranging the chunks in a design. "Thanks," she said, helping herself.

Jack settled in across from her and watched as she ate. He no longer looked like he was attending a board meeting. He was wearing a pair of khaki pants and white T-shirt. The pants had been clean and pressed this morning, but now they looked worn, almost dirty. His hair was tousled and he still hadn't shaved. "So," she said, "what did you do today? Buy a few countries?"

"I fixed something for you."

She set down her tea, surprised. Just that morning he was so anxious to leave that he was going to burrow his way out. Now he was helping her fix things? "I thought you were working."

"I did some, but without being able to go online...well,

there was only so much I could do. And I found that it was difficult to concentrate with you reading your articles out loud.''

"Sorry," she said. "You could've asked me to be quiet."

"Not at all. It was interesting to hear how you work. You were always a great writer."

She sighed. "Just not a good businesswoman."

"Math was never your strong suit, no. But you can't have everything," he added cheerfully.

"No," she said, "you certainly can't." But she wasn't thinking of the paper anymore. She was thinking about Jack.

"By the way," she said, "the phone is back on. In case you want to go online now."

He shook his head. "No. I'm actually enjoying my little break from the office. It's been a long time since I took a vacation."

"This hardly qualifies as a vacation," she said. "No heat or electricity. Freezing cold with no warm water…"

He laughed. "It shows you what I've had to settle for, doesn't it?"

She picked up a piece of bread and offered it to him. "I can't imagine you settling, Jack."

He took the bread. "What about you, Katie? When's the last time you went on vacation?"

She thought for a while and then said, "I guess my honeymoon. Matt and I went to Niagara Falls."

"Oh, yeah." She saw him grimace. "What made you decide to go there?"

"My parents went there for their honeymoon. I guess I was thinking that, well, if we went there, it would make us more like them. It might help our marriage."

"Help your marriage? It was your honeymoon."

"I wanted to love him like my mother loved my father. I thought that love was something you could control. Something that could be turned on and off. I've since learned that it's not." She shifted her eyes back to the fire. "So," she said, "fill me in on your life. I heard you went to Yale for grad school."

"Yes," he said.

"And after you graduated?"

He laughed. "Boring and more boring."

"Look at you," she said. "You have your own building. Full of people that work for you."

"And so do you."

"But mine is in a small town," she said. "Besides, I inherited mine. You made yours."

He shrugged. "Hard work. And luck. I got in with a very smart guy, and when he wanted to retire I bought him out. I had some lucky investments and my name got around. I hired talented people to bring in business. Everything, for lack of a better word, snowballed."

"You make it sound easy."

"I didn't have any distractions."

"That's not what I've heard."

He got up and threw another log into the fire. "I don't think they count as distractions unless love is involved."

"I find it hard to believe that it wasn't."

"What?" he asked, turning back toward her.

"I know you, Jack." She stood up and sat on the couch. "You're hard-nosed and stubborn, but you're still a romantic under it all."

He laughed. "You think you're so smart." He closed the fire screen and sat back down next to her. His leg was touching hers, his hand grazed her arm. He smelled like salt mixed with earth. It was a natural, hearty, masculine scent.

Butterflies began to swirl in her stomach. This was beginning to feel like a date, she thought. As if she could remember how that felt.

"What are you thinking about?" he asked, his voice low and soft.

"I'm thinking that it's nice having you here. Spending time with you again."

"I feel the same way," he said.

Once again she wanted to ask him why he had dropped her out of the blue, why he had no longer wanted to be her friend. But the moment passed and she was left with the warm, hazy feeling of the here and now. She was with Jack, for whatever reason, and she should enjoy it while it lasted.

"I've missed you, Jack," she said.

He put his arm around her and gave her shoulders a little squeeze.

"So," she said, "what did you fix?"

"Eat and I'll show you."

She tucked another piece of cheese inside her mouth and said, "I'm ready."

He took her hand and pulled her up, then grabbed her jacket and held it out for her.

"Outside?" she asked.

"Outside," he replied, assisting her with her jacket.

He pulled on his coat and nodded toward the back door.

Katie stepped outside and stopped. In the gathering darkness the shed that looked about ready to fall down was standing straight up for the first time in years, its broken side firm and straight.

"Jack," she breathed.

"Come on." He took her by the hand and led her to the shed. Brand-new beams ran across the ceiling. The corner posts had been repaired, as well. "You did all this?" she asked.

"It's been a while since I've built anything, but it all came back to me. Plus, I was here when your dad built this shed. He explained how to support the roof."

"And you remembered? Good heavens!"

"Sure," he said. Looking her straight in the eye he said, "It's kind of like riding a bike. Once you learn how, you never forget."

She felt her heart flutter and she took a step forward, toward him. Once again she thought about the way his fingers had felt on her skin. *Maybe I can help you relax....*

But she had pushed him away. The man she had desired since she could remember had finally offered seduction and she had spurned him.

"Jack," she said. "About what happened this morning..."

Jack held up his hand. "Forget it," he said. "I don't know what I was thinking."

Katie's heart sank. She had gotten a chance. And she had choked.

"Come on," he said. "This isn't your only surprise." He grabbed the lapels of her coat and said, "Button up. We need to walk around the house."

Katie buttoned her coat, too stunned to say anything else. When she was finished, Jack put his arm around her shoulder and led her out of the shed. They walked through the snow, neither speaking. As they approached the garage, Jack said, "Close your eyes."

She stood in the snow, waiting. Suddenly she heard a familiar noise—her car purring to life for the first time in weeks. She opened her eyes. "You fixed my car!"

"I had no choice. I knew you'd never let me buy you a new one."

"But how?" she said, walking into the garage. "What was wrong?"

"You had a couple of lousy connections. And the carburetor still needs to be replaced. But at least the car's drivable."

Jack smiled. The light over his head framed him in a warm, rosy glow. She felt as if she was having a beautiful dream.

"I don't know what to say," she said.

"You don't have to say anything." He smiled. "It felt good to work with my hands again. It's been a while since I spent a day like this."

"Well, I appreciate it. It was very kind of you."

He shrugged. Praise had always made Jack uncomfortable. "It was nothing."

He turned and walked out of the garage, his hands tucked in his pockets. Katie turned off the car and ran after him. "Jack," she said. "Why do you always walk away?"

Jack stopped and turned around. "What?"

She stood in front of him. "You still walk away. Just like you used to. Whenever anyone gives you a compliment, or tells you something nice, like how much they care, you leave."

He took another step toward her. "I never intended to walk away from you." He looked at her for a moment, his blue eyes smoldering. "What should I do now, Katie?"

He was moving slowly toward her, like a predator circling its prey. He was so close she could feel his breath against her cheek. Leaning over, his hands still in his pockets, he whispered, "What?"

She turned her head slightly and their lips touched.

Jack held his mouth against hers, long enough to whisper, "Tell me."

It was more than she could resist. She stopped breathing. He was against her now, his lips searching for more. Her brain stopped working as her heart responded. She cupped Jack's face and her lips received him.

The result was an explosion more intense than anything she had ever imagined. She had fantasized about this moment her whole life. But nothing had prepared her for the reality. Every sense sprang to life, every ounce of her tingling with desire. Standing there, in the middle of nowhere, she became lost in a haze of emotion. She could focus on one thought only. She loved Jack. And she always had.

As if in a dream she heard herself moan slightly when he slipped his tongue inside her mouth. He took his hands out of his pockets and tucked them behind her, receiving her fully as he drew her closer. She felt the warmth of his tongue as he teased her, tickling her tongue and exploring her mouth.

His hands slid inside her shirt. They began moving slowly

up her back, his fingers branding her with their touch as they
slid toward her bra.

She pressed herself against him, the hardness against her
leg encouraging her. Her heart beating wildly she rubbed up
against him. Gone was the good girl.

It no longer mattered if Jack loved her or not. She could
not think about the future. All she knew was that she needed
him—she wanted him. And she would settle for passion, if
only for a night. She was suddenly a temptress, determined
to receive satisfaction.

"Jack," she said, as her lips kissed their way over his
cheek, heading toward his ear. "I want you."

Jack stopped and stepped back.

It was as if she had hit him in the head with a snowball
again. After a split second of silence, she started talking as
fast as she could. "I know what it's all about and I know it
can never be anything, but I want you and I—"

"Katie," he said. He put his finger on her lips, quieting
her. "Let's go inside."

What the hell was going on here? Jack's head was spinning,
torn in a civil war. Part of him wanted to pull down her pants
and take her right there. The other wanted to give her a pat
on the head and make her another cup of tea. This morning
she'd wanted nothing to do with him. Yet now she was ready
to make love. Why? Because he had shown her some kindness
by helping her? Was she mistaking gratefulness for passion?
Did she think he expected to be repaid?

Jack's stomach turned at the thought. Or was it something
else, something that she'd mentioned? She had said she married Matt because she was going through a difficult time. She
had been confused. Well, she was certainly going through a
difficult time right now. He had no doubt that she was confused this time, as well.

Jack ran a hand through his hair. This was not the way it
was supposed to be. He wanted Katie, wanted her badly. But

not like this. He wanted it to be special, for her sake. Katie the romantic deserved that. She deserved more than just a quick hop in the hay. She deserved…romance and commitment. Just like she had said this morning.

But was he ready to commit? Hell, until a couple of days ago, he had assumed their relationship was over. Katie was to forever be a thorn stuck in his side. He had plans, major deals from which he could not afford to be distracted. He was moving to Europe, for God's sake. It had been in motion for years. How could he sleep with Katie and then walk away from her again? He couldn't do that to her. He couldn't do that to himself.

They were kidding themselves, thinking they could start over. If indeed, that was what she was thinking. But perhaps not. Perhaps he was flattering himself. Maybe Katie's intentions were more primitive. She had been without a man for a while…perhaps she was just looking for sex.

If so, could he? Of course he could. He had been attracted to Katie for as long as he could remember. So why not? They were both consenting adults.

They reached the door. "I'll be right back," Katie said, giving his hand a squeeze. Heat surged through him as he avoided her eyes.

He walked over to the fire and threw in another log. He glanced at her computer. It was still there, on the couch, just where she had left it. He closed it up and paused. Once again he thought of *The Falls*. Of her struggle to save the town she loved.

This was Katie, for God's sake. Not some anonymous woman. He couldn't go through with this. He couldn't make love to her and walk away again.

He glanced up. Katie was standing in front of him, wearing a sheer white gown. The moon hit her hair, making her once again look like an angel heaven-sent. The gauzy material floated around her lithe body. Unable to look away, he gazed at her, admiring her full, ripe breasts and the deep color of her perfect, round nipples. Her lean, tight belly. Legs that went on forever.

Jack inhaled deeply. He had been with some of the most beautiful women in the world, but not one of them could hold a candle to Katie.

Katie took a step toward him. "How do I look?" he heard her ask. Her voice quivered slightly, betraying her nerves. The effect was as intoxicating as her gown.

He swallowed. This was not going to be easy. "Nice," he said as his eyes ran over her once more.

"Just nice?" she asked. She was in front of him now. Close enough for him to feel the warmth of her sweet breath. Close enough for him to smell her lemon-scented skin. "Kiss me, Jack."

But he couldn't. Or could he? Just one kiss…one kiss and then…

Their lips touched, and Jack felt the fire erupt inside him, take control of his mind. The heat surged into a passion so intense he couldn't think of anything else. His hand cupped her rear as he pulled her toward him. She slid into the crook of his arm, her head resting against his shoulder. His tongue slipped into her mouth, circling and exploring. She was an elixir more potent than life itself. If he didn't stop now he wouldn't be able to.

He reached his hand up and touched her breast, moaning slightly as he felt her nipples harden under his touch. He wanted to consume her. He'd settle for nothing less.

Like a woman skilled in seduction, Katie sank down on the carpet. She held out her hand in an invitation to join her.

He took her hand and dropped down to his knees, directly in front of the crackling fire. He could see the rapid movement of her chest, pounding with each breath. He knew she was nervous. But he also knew he couldn't stop now, even if he wanted to. A lifetime of desire demanded satisfaction.

Katie felt like a schoolgirl about to lose her virginity. She forgot about Matt. She forgot about her history with Jack. All she cared about was the here and now. She took Jack's hand and held it to her heart. She led it down over her breasts, down toward the vee at the top of her legs.

Jack leaned forward, his eyes searing into hers. They reflected a fire and need so intense, she knew at that moment it was too late to turn back. But it didn't matter. She had been waiting for this moment for a long time.

Jack pressed his lips to hers, engulfing her in a kiss so intense, it made her dizzy. As he pulled her toward him, she reveled in the iron strength of his arms.

With his lips still pressed against her, she lay down flat on the floor.

He paused, taking a moment to study her. He touched her cheek, rolling his finger down toward her chin. "You're so beautiful," he said. He ran his finger over her gown, over her breasts and across her belly.

Then he bent over her, taking one nipple in his mouth as he sucked through the gown. His mouth retraced the path his fingers had just blazed, kissing her down around her belly. He took his time, caressing her with his tongue and fingers as if slowly unwrapping a present. Just when she was getting desperate to feel him against her bare skin, she felt him reach under her gown. She held her breath as his fingers began working their way up her inner thigh, toward her most intimate part.

He found her soft folds of flesh and ran a finger over and around, taking his time as he explored. Katie arched her hips, pressing herself against him, unable to stop. Jack pushed his finger inside, feeling his way through her dark wetness. With his skilled fingers still working, his mouth once again retraced their steps, kissing her inner thighs before taking over for his fingers, probing and searching. He ran his tongue up over her peak and back down again, gently caressing her.

"Now, Jack, please," she said, reaching for the top of his pants and unzipping them.

Jack closed his eyes as she touched him, emitting a low, guttural sound of pleasure. She pulled out his hard, heavy shaft, her hands wrapped around it like a treasured object. She ran her fingers up and down before Jack stopped her. Pinning her hands above her head, he pushed into her, deep and slow.

A lightning rod of warmth spread through her, a tingling sensation from her head to her toes. Katie wrapped her legs around him even more tightly as she arched her back. With each thrust the pressure built. Katie stared at the handsome face she had loved for so long. Jack's brow was furrowed and his breath tight as he attempted to control his lust. It excited her even more to see the effects of the pleasure her body was giving to him. "Don't stop," she heard herself plead. Jack went even deeper, their bodies synchronized in passion.

As the fierce threat of release rose to a fiery peak, Katie closed her eyes. Jack let go of her hands and she held him to her, her fingernails digging in his skin. Then, with a cry, the first wave flooded through her. As she convulsed against him she could feel Jack shudder and groan, pulling her even deeper.

Afterward, Katie stared up into the eyes of the man who had haunted her dreams for as long as she could remember. All her emotions were raw and spent. Making love with Jack had been everything she had hoped. But as a result, she was vulnerable, exposed, and even more open to pain.

"Katie," Jack whispered. He pulled her to him. "Are you all right?" Jack felt as if his mind was going in a million different directions. And now it looked as if Katie was about to cry.

"I'm fine," she said, but he knew instinctively it was not the truth. She nestled her head in the crook of his arm and she wrapped her arms around his neck. He could feel the tears against his neck. He took her arms and pulled her away, so that he could see her.

"You're crying."

She laughed and turned away, as if embarrassed. "They're good tears. I didn't expect it to be so…intense."

How could he have allowed this to happen? It was too much, too soon, dammit. "Katie, I'm sorry." He held her to him once again.

"Don't be sorry," she said. "It's just that, well, you're the only man I've been with besides Matt."

She wasn't crying because of him, but because of Matt. Jack felt his blood run cold. He was glad Katie hadn't been with anyone else, but he would've been a lot happier if Matt had never entered the picture. Despite what Katie had said about their passionless marriage, he guessed his old nemesis still held a piece of her heart. Matt may have disappeared from her life, but his presence was still felt.

Jack heard himself say, "I don't know what to say."

She smiled and ran her finger around his lips. "Don't worry," she said. "I don't have any expectations."

Jack felt like he had just been derailed. "What?"

"Meaning I'm not comparing us to me and Matt. You and I are friends. Nothing more."

He got the picture. She cared about him, sure. Not enough to marry him. Not enough to wait for him. But enough to sleep with him.

Perfect, right? Isn't this the kind of relationship he preferred? Sex without consequences. No hard feelings. No strings attached.

"Jack?" she said. "Did I say something wrong? I just didn't want you to worry. I'm a big girl. I know what this is."

"Oh?"

She outlined his chin with her finger. "One night."

A night, Jack thought, he would never forget. And that was the problem.

Jack broke away from her. He stood up and pulled his pants back on. "You should change into something warmer," he said. "You don't want to freeze."

Katie looked away.

Jack yanked his shirt over his head, then reached out to pull her up. He dropped her hand, yet Katie didn't move. She stood before him, naked.

For one split second he was tempted to change his mind. To push her onto the couch and make love to her yet again.

But he couldn't. If he did, he would never be able to stop himself from telling her exactly how he felt, and that was something she obviously did not want to hear. No, he thought. He had to forget about what just happened. He had to turn off his emotions just as he had managed to turn them off years ago. "Go on, Katie," he said, turning away and nodding toward the door. "You'll get cold."

Only after she was gone did he allow himself to breathe.

Seven

Katie was not ready to wake up. She was having a dream, a wonderful dream. She was with Jack, someplace warm, some place exotic. They were in a tent, all alone. She could hear the rhythmic sounds of the ocean as they kissed....

She opened her eyes. She realized that it was not the ocean she was hearing, but Jack. She was lying on top of him, her arms wrapped tightly around his neck. Her sweatshirt was hiked up and Jack's hands were resting on her bare back, right where her bra strap was supposed to be.

She stayed still for a moment, afraid to move, or even breathe. What in the world had happened? How had she managed to crawl on top of him like this? She was mortified, afraid he would wake and see what she had done. She thought back to the previous night. After they had made love, Jack had changed. She had half expected it, knowing him as she did. She knew he would be concerned that once they made love, she would expect a relationship. And of course, she had started crying, which hadn't helped.

She wished she could turn back time and live that moment over again. This time she wouldn't cry. She wouldn't allow herself to think about how she had finally experienced just the type of fireworks she had read about in books. And she wouldn't allow herself to realize she would never feel the same way about another man. And last, but not least, she wouldn't try to alleviate his concerns by pretending she was thinking about Matt.

It had been afterglow, Katie-style. Awkward and stiff. She had blown it.

Still, she had not been prepared for the cruel and casual way he had dismissed her. How could he do that—make love and then toss her away as if she were yesterday's news?

But that was what he had done. He'd treated her as she suspected he treated all of his women. He was interested in the catch, but not in the consequences. She'd looked into his cold, dead eyes and realized the passion that had seemed eternal only moments earlier was gone for good.

So she had gone back upstairs and changed into her old sweats. She felt humiliated…almost used. But what did she expect? He had warned her to stay away. But she couldn't seem to help herself. Never before had she been so forward with a man. What was she thinking?

It was that kiss, that amazing kiss. The way his tongue felt in her mouth, the way it felt to be pressed against him… It had been intoxicating. And she had acted as if she was drunk. She had thrown all her cares and precautions to the wind and gone for it. And she had been shot down.

She didn't know how she would face him. What in the world would they talk about? If she wouldn't have frozen to death, she would've considered sleeping upstairs. Fortunately, by the time she'd come back down, Jack was on the couch, asleep. At the sight of him she could feel all her anger melt away. He looked so endearing, his arms crossed against his chest, and his black hair lopping over his eye. It was as if sleep had metamorphosed him back into her sweet friend. She had tucked a pillow under his head and covered him with a blanket. Then she'd settled in on the opposite end of the sofa

She had sat there for what seemed like hours. But at some point, she must've fallen asleep and crawled on top of him. The mere thought of it was mortifying.

She had no choice but to extricate herself from an embarrassing situation. She began to slowly twist away. Jack's breathing skipped a beat, then he sighed, and she thought he was going to remove his hands. Instead, they slid down her coming to a rest on either side of her chest. If his thumb moved a fraction, it would be on her bare breast. And that wasn't all. She could feel something else pressing against her too. His manhood was big and firm, poking through his jeans and up against her belly. She knew he was sleeping, knew that it wasn't because of her or anything she did, but still…

"Good morning, Katie."

She was so surprised, she nearly rolled over onto the ground. He steadied her, his thumb grazing into the forbidden zone. With her heart in her throat, she said, "I was just…I guess I…"

He smiled, staring directly into her eyes. It was enough to send shivers back down her spine.

"Cold?" he asked.

She shook her head. He still hadn't made any attempt to break free.

"Then why are you shivering?"

"I'm just, um, hungry."

"So am I," he said, not taking his eyes off her.

They were distracted by the ringing of his phone. She used the opportunity to pick herself up. She yanked her sweatshirt down, reached over and handed him his phone.

He sighed and then flipped it open and said, "Yes?"

Katie stood up and walked over to the fire. She opened the screen and tossed in another log.

"Okay," Jack said. "Sorry, Carol…"

Carol, she thought as a chill ran though her. So she was

his girlfriend, after all. Why else would she call first thing in the morning? She was probably calling to find out where he'd spent the night and with whom.

"I don't know when I'm getting back," she heard Jack continue. "I know, I know. It's going to have to wait. There's nothing I can do about it now, is there?" he said, agitated.

She remembered how she felt when she discovered Matt was with another woman. Even though she hadn't loved him, the betrayal still stung. She'd sworn she would never inflict that kind of pain on anyone. But apparently, she had.

When he shut the phone, she asked, "Is she all right?"

"Carol?" He shrugged. "She'll get over it."

She stood up, miffed that he could be so casual about it. Didn't he feel the least guilty?

Jack walked over to her and put his hand on her shoulder. "Katie," he said. "I think we should talk about last night."

"There's nothing to talk about," she said. "And I apologize to Carol. I had no business—"

"Why would you apologize to Carol?"

"I know what if feels like to be with a man who's... unfaithful."

Jack looked confused. "What in hell are you—" He stopped. After a beat he said, "Do you... You don't think that Carol and I...?"

She raised her eyebrows.

"Carol?" He smiled. "Carol works for me. She's my accountant. She's a wonderful woman, however her husband of forty years and her children and grandchildren might not be too happy to hear about our affair."

A wave of relief rushed through her. "So you're not seeing anyone?"

He shook his head. "No."

She stepped back, away from him. "Not that it's any of my business."

He took another step toward her. "For the record, I've

never been unfaithful to anyone in my life. I would never d
that to you or anyone else.''

Their eyes locked. For a moment, Katie felt the familia
pull at her heart. She wanted to kiss him. To hold him. T
possess him.

Instead, she spun around and grabbed her jacket.

''Where are you going?'' Jack asked.

''To get more wood.''

''I'll do it.''

''Not necessary,'' Katie replied, tugging on her boots. She
wanted to get away from him. Anywhere would do.

She practically ran out the door, but she paused when she
stepped outside. Another foot of snow had fallen overnight
Fresh powder coated everything, turning her yard into a mag
ical-looking forest. When she took a step, the snow came up
to her knee. She glanced at the sky. The worst was over
Although it was still overcast, it was warmer and the snow
had withered to a flurry. They would be able to get out soon
And Jack would be able to leave.

At the thought of him going, her heart sank. She wondered
when she would see him again. Don't do this, she warned
herself. Stop.

She promised herself their lovemaking would not turn her
into some crazy woman possessed by love. But, she realized
her feelings had little to do with sex. It was Jack.

She had forgotten how much she enjoyed spending time
with him. It had been so nice talking to him again…playing
with him. For the first time since she could remember, she
had actually had moments where she hadn't thought about
work.

Brushing the snow off the shed door, once again she ad
mired Jack's work. It had warmed her heart that he had cared
enough to help. She swallowed and gave the door another
yank.

The door wouldn't budge. She pushed some snow aside
clearing a path for the door. She tugged again. Still nothing

he began pulling harder, using all her force to open it. After
ne particularly big yank, she let go, flung backward, straight
to Jack's arms.

"Easy does it," he said into her ear. "I told you I would
elp."

She jumped away, flustered. "I can get it," she said. "Be-
des, you're not even wearing boots."

"I did this yesterday, remember?" he said, moving past
er. He started kicking the snow away from the door. A blast
f snow flew right at Katie, covering her from head to toe.
ack's face broke into a broad grin.

Katie smiled, but as she looked at Jack, her good humor
ded. He was casual and relaxed, acting as if nothing had
appened the night before. As if the earth had not moved and
e heavens had not opened up. They were back to being
riends.

Katie could almost feel her heart breaking. What had she
one? She would never be able to go back to being just
riends. Never.

"Sorry," he said. "It was an accident—" But his apology
as never finished.

For Katie turned and ran back into the house.

Dammit! Jack thought. This was not what he had intended.
e'd intended to make love to Katie the minute she opened
er eyes, but the phone had interrupted his plans. And now
he was doing everything she could to stay away from him.
Ie couldn't blame her. He'd acted like an idiot the night
efore, practically pushing her away, right after she'd given
erself to him.

But what else could he have done? He couldn't stand to
eel her once again, knowing that she would never be his. *You
nd I are friends,* she had said. *Nothing more.*

He was a fool to have even thought otherwise. After all, it
ad been years since the day she had expressed her love.
ince then she had married his best friend. Still, he had har-

bored a hope that perhaps they might be able to turn bac
time. To pick up where they'd left off that day at the creek

He had lain awake thinking about his predicament f
hours, his body arguing one side, his heart another. Eve
when Katie came back downstairs and had sweetly given hi
a pillow and blanket, he could feel what was now the famili
tightening in his groin. Part of him desired nothing more tha
to pull her down on top of him and pick up where they le
off. Unfortunately, at that point in time, he still wasn't su
he could make love on her terms.

But long after Katie had fallen asleep, Jack had come to a
important realization. It didn't matter how Katie felt abo
him. What mattered was how he felt about her. And, as a ma
in love, he had an obligation to make her happy. To plea
her. But first, he needed to ask her to forgive him.

Jack started walking faster. If she forgave him, he woul
give her the sex of a lifetime, he would give her the firework
she had requested. And whenever she desired, they would g
their separate ways.

He opened the door. "Katie?" he called.

"There's power again," she said from upstairs. "I'm sur
Burt will be over soon to plow us out."

Katie was still talking. He recognized it as a product o
nervousness, talking fast about everything and anything. "
you want to take a shower, go right ahead," she continue
"I just got out. The water's pretty cold, but bearable. I le
you some extra towels next to the sink."

She had just gotten out of the shower. The thought of Kati
wet and naked, was enough to make him instantly hard. H
took the stairs two at a time. Her closed bedroom door didn
stop him. Without knocking, he walked into her room.

Katie was standing in front of him, her back toward him
She was wearing bikini panties and struggling to latch he
bra. At the sound of him she dropped her bra and crossed he
arms in front of her naked breasts.

"Jack?" She whipped around. Her hair was wet and un

combed. "The bathroom is that way," she said, pointing behind him.

He gazed at her delicate shoulders, followed the curve of
her slender belly down to her perfect rear end. She was in
amazing shape, not an ounce of fat on her. He thought of how
she had felt this morning, her full breasts resting up against
him. His reaction was immediate, his need for her intense.

"I came to apologize," he said, walking slowly toward her.

"For what?"

"The way I acted last night. Asking you to get dressed…"

"There's no need to apologize," she said, attempting to
step away.

But Jack was too fast. He gently took her in his arms and
held her from behind. "Forgive me, Katie," he whispered in
her ear. "Please."

He slid his hands under her bra and cupped her breasts. She
arched her back like a kitten enjoying a toy.

When he slid his hand down inside her panties, his fingers
touching the soft folds of her most private part, she gasped
with pleasure and leaned her head back against his chest. The
lavender scent of her hair, the clean, fresh smell of her skin
were more enticing than any perfume.

"I want to make you feel good, Katie." He slid one finger
inside her. She was wet and warm. Her hands reached over
her head and around his neck, giving him a nook to nuzzle.

"Hey, Katie," a man yelled from downstairs. "Are you all
right?"

Katie jumped away from Jack and grabbed her sweats. "It's
Burt," she whispered to Jack. Then she called out, "I'm
fine."

Jack smiled. Old Burt Weasley. What terrible timing. Jack
walked toward the door.

"Where are you going?" Katie asked, talking in a loud
whisper.

"To say hello to Burt," Jack said.

"No!" Katie tried to stop him, but Jack just smiled and

kept going. As far as he was concerned, there was nothing to be embarrassed about. They weren't children caught necking. They were grown adults who knew exactly what they were doing.

"Whose car is stuck at the end of the drive there…" Burt was continuing. He stopped as he saw Jack. "Oh, geesh," he said, his mouth dropping in surprise. "You've got company. Sorry about that. I didn't mean to intrude."

Katie's heart was going a mile a minute. As she tripped into her pants, she couldn't help but think about Jack's fingers on her breasts.

But she didn't have time to dwell on it. Burt had caught them together. And Burt's wife was an incorrigible gossip. Katie knew the news of her being alone with a strange man would spread through Newport Falls like wildfire. Katie yanked a sweatshirt over her head and dashed out of the room.

"Burt," she exclaimed, "this isn't company. This is Jack Reilly. You remember Jack." Burt Weasley was eighty years old. He had been plowing Katie's driveway for as long as she was alive. His eyes narrowed as he looked at Jack carefully.

Jack stuck out his hand. "Good to see you again, Mr. Weasley." Katie couldn't help but notice that Jack looked amused. It was as if he was enjoying this awkward moment.

"You, too, Jack," Burt said. "I heard you were back in town. But I didn't know you were staying with our friend Katie here."

"He's not," Katie said quickly. "He was staying at the inn. But he drove me home in the blizzard and his car— Well, that car at the end of the driveway? That's his."

"You got yourself pretty stuck," Burt said to Jack. "Bet they don't have this kind of snow in the city, huh?"

Jack smiled. "No, sir. They certainly don't."

"I plowed around you," Burt said. "Got up real close. Why don't you start your car and I'll give you a pull out." He kicked some snow off his boots. "Once you get going, though, you're not going to be able to stop. You should be okay if you go straight up the road and to the expressway." He cleared his throat and said, "Unless, of course, you were planning on staying a while."

"No," Katie said to Burt. "I know Jack is anxious to leave."

"I am?" Jack said, looking at Katie. The smile faded. "But we have some unfinished business."

Katie felt dizzy. What did he mean? That he wanted more...of her?

"Son," Burt said, "if you plan on getting out before spring, now's the time."

Jack stood still, looking at Katie, as if waiting for her to say something. But what did he want her to say?

"Okay," Jack said finally. "Thanks, Burt. I'll grab my things."

"You're welcome." Burt glanced from Katie to Jack. "I'll be outside."

When Burt left, Katie turned back to Jack. She laughed nervously and said, "By noon it'll be all over town that you and I spent a romantic winter holiday together."

"Is that a problem?" Jack asked. He took another step toward her.

Not for you, Katie felt like saying. You're going to leave and I'll probably never see you again....

"I want you to come to New York," he said.

Katie felt her heart soar. He wanted to see her again.

He took her hand and held it. "There's a meeting tomorrow night. It's a dinner, actually, and a lot of key people from my board will be there. I think it would be a good idea for you to be there. You can talk to them yourself. Tell them about the merits of having a business in Newport Falls."

Katie stared at his fingers, entwined with hers. This had nothing to do with him not wanting to part; this was business. Her business. So why was he holding her hand? "You want me to pitch your board?" she asked hoarsely.

"Sort of," he said. He squeezed her hand and then let it go, walking into the other room. "Look, Katie, this is going to take a lot more than I originally thought. And I'll be quite honest with you. It's a long shot."

She nodded. "Okay."

Jack came out of the living room carrying his briefcase. He set it down, pulled his coat off the banister and shrugged it on. "Be at the airport at four o'clock tomorrow afternoon. Go to hangar B and tell them you're traveling on my jet. Greg will see that you get to the city." He opened the door. He waved at Burt and then came back over to her. "Oh, and you better pack some clothes. Plan on spending the night." He touched her chin with his black-gloved hand. "As I said, we have quite a lot of unfinished business." And with a grin on his handsome face, he left.

Eight

Katie had a hard time focusing on work the next day. Still, she made it through, and at three o'clock sharp, she and Marcella left for the airport. Jack's pilot was waiting for her when she arrived. Greg was a cheery-looking redhead who grabbed her luggage and walked her to the plane. He introduced her to the flight attendant, Cary, and took his seat at the controls.

Katie had never been on a private plane before, she'd never even flown first class. But she couldn't imagine anything more luxurious than this. There were soft leather seats, set up like a living room, and a big-screen TV. Cary's only job, it appeared, was to wait on her. He immediately offered her champagne, which she accepted.

The luxury was almost overwhelming. She had to give Jack credit. He had done this all by himself, with no help from family. The boy who was once so poor he couldn't afford a bike now owned his own plane. She couldn't imagine having so much money.

She leaned back in the comfortable seat and stared at the clouds, trying desperately to relax.

But it was difficult. Ever since Jack had left, she'd been unable to stop thinking about him. She could still feel his touch on her bare skin, still feel the warmth of his fingers running down her back....

She took a sip of the champagne, the bubbles tingling in her mouth. She swallowed and closed her eyes, and once again saw herself half-naked, standing in her room. Like a delicious dream, she felt Jack behind her, pressed up against her.

She opened her eyes and sighed. How could she even pretend to focus on her meeting knowing the pleasure that awaited?

But she would have to focus. She had no choice. This was her business she was trying to save. Her family's newspaper. The whole town depended on her making this work. She had to ignore her personal feelings and concentrate on the matter at hand.

She knew Jack was going out on a limb for her and she appreciated it. She hoped she wouldn't disappoint him. She had spent the day pulling together some of the financials from her paper, and anything else she thought might help. Afterward she'd dashed home to throw some things in her suitcase. It hadn't taken her long to pack, simply because she had little to choose from. Most of her business clothes had years of wear. She barely had money for the necessities these days, none for frivolous items like clothes. She had settled on a simple black dress for the evening and a suit for tomorrow. And for tonight, she had packed a silk nightgown.

She took another sip of the champagne and closed her eyes as the warmth flooded through her veins. As the jet left her world far behind, her thoughts drifted between what she wanted to think about—making love to Jack—and what she should be thinking about—saving her business. In either case, she had no idea what she was in store for. All she could hope was that she was up to it.

Cary led her off the plane and carried her baggage to a waiting black limousine. He turned her over to the driver.

"I'm Ralph," he said, explaining that he had been Mr. Reilly's personal driver for five years.

So much for Jack taking cabs. "Do you know where we're going?" she asked. She realized she hadn't even asked Jack where he lived.

"To the Plaza."

The Plaza? She was staying at a hotel? She had just assumed that she would be staying with Jack. How could she have been so presumptuous? Not only was she embarrassed, she was going to a hotel she could not afford. She named an economy hotel chain. "Isn't there one on Thirty-fourth Street? I'd rather stay there."

"There's a huge convention, ma'am. I'm afraid unless you have reservations, you'll never get in this late."

"Mr. Reilly was able to get a room at the Plaza," she reminded Ralph.

"Mr. Reilly keeps a permanent room there."

"What?"

"For his visitors and his, um—" he cleared his throat "—guests." His eyes shifted back to her.

"Guests," she repeated. A current of jealousy ran through her as she thought of the women she had seen photographed with Jack. "Well, I'm sure he has a lot of those." As relieved as she was that he probably wouldn't expect her to pay, she was insulted she was getting the same treatment as the other women he associated with. But why would he treat her any differently?

She drew her lips tightly together. She had promised him and herself that she didn't have any expectations. Yet they had slept together only once and she was already feeling possessive.

When Ralph dropped her off in front of the hotel, she

checked in and went up to her room. It was a suite, consisting of a living room with a fireplace and a bedroom with a king-size bed. She walked around the bed, trying not to imagine how many times Jack had lain in it, his arms around another woman.

But as she glanced out the window, she forgot about the bed. The view of the sun setting on Central Park and the city beyond was breathtaking. When she could tear her eyes away, she noticed the Bloomingdale's bag on the dresser. Inside the bag was a large box. She opened the note on top of it.

Dear Ms. Devonworth,

Jack asked me to choose something for you to wear tonight. I hope this is suitable. I look forward to meeting you.

Carol Casey

P.S. Jack wanted to make it clear that you are under no obligation to wear this. It is merely a suggestion.

Jack knew she wouldn't have anything suitable to wear. He didn't want to be embarrassed by her.

She swallowed her feelings as she opened the box. The dress was blue, and strapless, with a satin top and a full skirt of layer upon layer of the softest chiffon she had ever seen. It was a dress suitable for a princess.

Jack walked through the lobby of the Plaza, past the Oak Bar to the elevators. He had been in this lobby many times before. Most of those times he had been there to pick up the dates waiting for him in the suite he kept at the hotel. But never had he been so nervous.

He straightened his tuxedo tie as he stepped into the elevator. He'd realized after he left Katie that the event was formal. But he didn't want her to worry about buying a dress. Better, he thought, to simply surprise her with one when she arrived. He knew she would never have allowed him to buy one for her. Katie was much too proud and stubborn to accept a gift from him.

He went over the itinerary he had planned so well. The ball, then a private dinner at Fachette. A tour of the city, then back here for a nightcap. And then... He smiled. He would make good on his promise. He would give Katie what she wanted—no strings attached.

He knocked on the door. He could hear the patter of feet and the door swung open.

Jack was too stunned to speak. He had never seen her, or any woman, look so beautiful. Her shoulder-length hair was pulled sleekly back. Her makeup was minimal. But the effect of the dress, the way it fit her and became her, was magical.

Katie grinned and waved. "Thanks for the loaner," she said. "I'll try not to spill." She brushed past him. "Ready?"

He grabbed her arm and stopped her. "Wait," he said. "Let me look at you." He gazed at her from head to foot, taking it all in. "You look beautiful."

"Thanks." She shrugged off his arm and kept walking.

"Katie," he said, stopping her once again. "What's wrong?"

"Nothing's wrong," she said, pressing the elevator button. "I appreciate you loaning me a dress."

"It's not a loan, it's a gift."

"I don't want a gift, but thank you."

"It's yours," he said quietly, with conviction.

She hesitated. In a quiet voice she said, "I understand why you got this for me. You knew I didn't have anything to wear that would be presentable and you didn't want me to embarrass myself. It was a kind gesture, but too generous."

"Katie, nothing you wear could possibly embarrass me. And no matter what you wear, you would still be the most beautiful woman in the room."

Katie stepped into the elevator, and Jack followed. Fortunately, they were alone. He said, "I got you this dress to please you."

She glanced at him. "Thank you."

Jack bit his tongue. This was not going according to plan. But then again, with Katie, things rarely did. "How is your room?"

"Fine," she said. "But had I known I would be staying at a hotel, I would've made my own accommodations."

Jack looked at her, surprised. "Where did you think you'd be?"

Katie blushed. She pushed the elevator button again.

He stopped as the truth dawned on him. She assumed she would be staying with him. She had *wanted* to stay with him.

"Katie, I just assumed you would want—"

"To be treated like all your other women," she said. The doors opened, and she stepped out before he could respond.

"Katie," Jack began, hurrying to catch up with her once again.

"It's okay," she said, holding up her hand. "I'm flattered to be in such glamorous company."

She whipped her shawl around her shoulders and started walking down the street. Jack stared after her. Where in the world did she think she was going? "Wait," he called out. "The car is right here."

"Oh." She turned around and, after pausing a moment to seemingly gather her dignity, marched back.

"Look," Jack said before she could escape into the car. He took her hands and held them. "You're Katie. You're special."

"I'm sorry," she said quietly. "I'm just uncomfortable about you spending money on me like this. "

"But I want to."

"It's just…difficult for me. You've changed and so have I. How could we not? Our situations are so different from when we were kids."

"I still see the same Katie. And just because I can afford my own dinner doesn't mean I've changed." He let go of her hands and opened the door. He felt as if he had been blindsided. He was trying to win her over, trying to make her happy. And he had done anything but. He should've known that Katie Devonworth wouldn't be impressed by fancy dresses and hotels.

"Come on," Jack said. "We don't want to be late."

He slid in beside her. He was thankful for Ralph, glad they were no longer alone.

"Hi, Ralph," she greeted him.

"Hello, Ms. Devonworth. You look very nice."

"Thanks, Ralph. You do, too."

Ralph had chauffeured many of Jack's dates. But not one of them had bothered talking to him. But then again, as he had just admitted, Katie was not one of his women. And it was looking like she never would be.

Katie sighed. What was she doing? Jack had been nothing but kind, yet here she was, giving him the third degree. She needed to keep her mouth shut and focus on business. "Maybe you should tell me what kind of event this is tonight."

"It's the annual midwinter ball."

"You're taking me to a ball! I thought it was a board dinner."

"It might as well be. Everyone on my board will be there. It's the perfect opportunity to talk to some people who have the ability to invest. I need you to sing the praises of Newport Falls."

"It's not hard to do," Katie said, surprised she could still speak. A ball? She was having a tough time focusing on the conversation. She needed to get it together. This, she reminded herself, was not a date. She may be dressed like a princess and he may have once been her Prince Charming, and they may be attending a ball, but technically, it was not a date.

"You always loved it there," Jack continued.

"Where?" Katie asked.

Jack looked at her. "Newport Falls, of course."

Katie was quiet. Jack was so eager to leave his old self behind, but she had loved the boy he was. She felt in disliking Newport Falls, he was denying a part of himself. And that was the part that belonged to her. "You liked it there once, too."

"Did I? I don't remember."

Katie crossed her arms. She was paying attention now. "The town certainly reached out to you."

"My statement had nothing to do with the town…or the people that lived there. It just wasn't a high point of my life."

Katie looked at the people waiting to cross the street. They seemed old and tired, as if prematurely aged by the city.

She glanced over at Jack. He was staring at her. This was not the lusty gaze he had focused on her earlier. He looked upset, as if the mere sight of her saddened him. What had she done? She had taken a perfectly nice evening and wrecked it.

"Okay," he said, "let's deal with the matter at hand."

She swallowed. "Okay." He was going to tell her that he'd changed his mind. He no longer wanted to be with her. He wanted her to go home by herself, to return to the small town she loved so much.

"At the ball," he said, "there's one man in particular I want you to talk to."

"Okay," Katie repeated, relieved.

"He's Franklin Bell of Bell Computers."

Bell Computers. Katie had heard of the company. It was one of the largest computer manufacturers in the country.

"They're currently based outside of New York, but they've run out of space. He's looking for a place to build a manufacturing plant. I think Newport Falls would be a good fit. His plants are clean, so pollution isn't a problem. It would bring people into the town and there would still be plenty of jobs left over for the unemployed."

"Sounds great," Katie breathed.

"But there's a problem."

"What?"

"He's already looked at Newport Falls and ruled it out."

"Why?"

"I'm not sure. That's your job. You need to find out why and convince him otherwise."

Bell Computers...Katie let her mind wander. If she could succeed in bringing a company like that to Newport Falls, the economy would get exactly the boost it needed. Suddenly she could see Main Street the way it had been in her youth, bustling with activity. Successful small businesses and coffee shops, packed with friends and neighbors.

"Well," said Jack, "we're here."

Despite his feelings about Newport Falls, he was still trying to save it. And he was trying to do so for her. So filled was she with gratitude, that she did the only thing she could think of. She kissed him.

At that moment Ralph opened the door. "Excuse me," he said.

Katie pulled away from Jack. "Oh, thank you, Ralph," she said. She stepped out, not looking back.

Jack touched his hand to his mouth. What in the hell was that? It was no ordinary kiss, either. No small peck of thank-you. It had been a full-frontal, lip-on-lip, smothering kiss. Enough to knock the wind out of him.

That was Katie. Spontaneous, full of life and surprises. Just when he was certain their evening was headed for disaster, she did a one-eighty. Until she kissed him he was beginning to think he had made a mistake inviting her to New York. Getting investors was a long shot, anyway. He would've been better off admitting the truth: he could not help her. Instead he had filled her with false hope and dragged her to the city, a place, obviously, she did not want to be.

Jack followed Katie out and grabbed her arm. "What was that?"

She smiled. "What?"

"That kiss."

But before Katie could answer, they were interrupted by a small, gray-haired woman. She glanced at Jack and said angrily, "You're late."

"What is it tonight?" Jack said. "I'm getting grief from all quarters."

"Don't even try to blame it on this lovely lady," the woman said. She looked at Katie, smiled and stuck out her hand. "I'm Carol Casey. And you're every bit as lovely as Jack said you were. I'm glad the dress fits. I sent one of Jack's assistants to get it."

"One of mine?" Jack asked.

"Mine were too busy, trying to put together this crazy deal. He's got us all working overtime for you, Katie."

"He has?" Katie asked. She turned back toward Jack and smiled. It was a smile of pure and total gratitude. He could feel himself melt. He'd been hoping to please her, to make her happy. He should've known there was only one way to do that. Katie turned back toward Carol and said, "I can't tell you how much I appreciate it. Thank you."

"Are you going inside?" Carol asked.

"Yes," Katie replied, all too quickly.

Katie and Jack kept their distance from each other as they walked through the crowded lobby and into the ballroom.

For a moment, Katie forgot about kissing Jack. She looked around her, amazed by the splendor. She had never seen anything so magnificent as this hotel ballroom. It was as if they had walked into a tropical oasis. Lighted palm trees were spaced throughout the huge room, while candles and tiki torches glowed in the dim lighting. A giant waterfall cascaded in the corner of the room and an orchestra played on stage.

Carol left and almost immediately they were greeted by an attractive, well-dressed elderly woman. "Jack," she said, shaking his hand. Then she turned toward Katie.

Jack said, "Eva, this is Katie Devonworth. Katie, this is Eva Bell. She's a member of my board."

"Nice to meet you," Katie said.

Eva shook her outstretched hand. "Jack told me you both grew up together in Newport Falls. I've heard of it, of course. But he neglected to mention how lovely you are. You're not single, are you, my dear?"

"Now, Eva," Jack said.

Katie laughed. "Yes, I am."

"Well," Eva said, "maybe you won't be by the end of the evening. Lord knows I've been trying to marry off Jack for years now. I think it's high time he settled down with the right woman, don't you?"

Katie could feel herself blush as her smile faded. She didn't want Jack settling down with anyone. Unless, of course, it was she.

"Eva," Jack said, "Katie is here for business, remember?"

"Of course," Eva replied. She turned back toward Katie and said, "Jack thinks my son Franklin might be able to help you."

"I hope so, too," Katie said.

"It's my job to introduce you." Eva turned around, glancing around the room. "Oh, there he is," she said, pointing to a handsome, if slightly rotund, fair-haired man.

"Well, Jack?" Eva said, looking back at him as she grabbed Katie's arm. "I think it's time they met, don't you?" She took Katie's hand and led her toward him.

Katie stopped thinking about Jack as she suddenly felt the pressure of the moment. It was as if the whole town, her whole universe, was depending on her performance. And she wasn't sure she was up to the task.

Katie turned back and glanced at Jack. "Good luck," he said. "You'll do fine."

It was the way he said it that touched her heart. She could tell that he really did think she was capable of wooing an immensely successful businessman. Jack had faith in her, and at that moment, that was all she needed. She was ready to save the day.

Eva tapped her son on the shoulder. "Franklin?" she said. Franklin turned around. "This is Katie Devonworth. I told you about her. She's from Newport Falls."

"Ah, yes," he said. He looked about as interested as if someone had just told him they were offering free bowling lessons. "The small-town editor."

"Publisher," Katie said crisply.

"Eva," Jack interrupted, taking the elderly woman by the arm. He nodded toward the orchestra and said, "Isn't this one of your favorite songs?"

"Why, yes," she said, tucking her arm into his. "It is."

Katie felt the anxiety swirl up and consume her as she watched Jack walk away.

"I hate these things," Franklin said.

"Don't worry," she said. "I'll be quick." She would say her spiel and get out of his way.

He looked at her curiously. "I was talking about the ball."

The ball. Of course. She was tempted to smack her head but she thought better of it. "Right," she said.

"So," he said suspiciously, "this is not a chance meeting, is it?"

Katie didn't skip a beat. She couldn't lie, even if it was for her benefit. "No."

He studied her for a moment. Then he said, "You already know that I own a company that makes computers. You know we're currently looking to expand, which means we need to move our manufacturing plant."

"Yes," she said.

"Then I'm afraid you're wasting your time. We looked at Newport Falls and rejected it."

"I know."

"So why are you here?"

She glanced over at Jack, but she couldn't see him. He had

disappeared into the crowd. "I'm asking myself that same question."

"Well, Miss Devonwright—"

"Devonworth."

"Whatever. I can't remember why we rejected Newport Falls, but I'm sure we had our reasons." He began to walk away.

"It's not for everyone," she called out. "Some people don't mind breathing polluted, dirty air. They don't mind having to worry about their children's safety when they walk to school or down the street. They don't mind dealing with people they can't trust, knowing that they could fall off the earth and it would be months before anyone would notice."

He turned around. "You're an unusual lobbyist, Ms. Devonworth."

"I'm not a lobbyist. I'm a newspaperwoman. And I've lived in Newport Falls my whole life. It's got everything. Mountains, water, clean air, nice neighbors. A real, old-fashioned Main Street…"

Katie went on and on. By the time she was finished, she needed a glass of water. He was leaning in, looking at her and smiling.

"That was quite a monologue."

"I get a little carried away," she said.

"It's nice to hear," he said. "It's hard to find people these days who are so passionate about where they live."

The orchestra started up again. Jack was still on the dance floor, but he was no longer dancing with Eva. Instead, he was now with a beautiful blonde. Franklin shook his head and grinned. "Look at your date. Up to no good as usual."

Jealousy once again stabbed her heart. "He's not my date," Katie said quickly.

"No?" he asked.

Or was he? After all, he was paying for her hotel room. And it was almost certain they would wake up side by side. Unless, of course, he got a better offer. "He's an old friend."

At that moment, Jack and the woman turned and looked at her. The woman winked.

Franklin held out his hand to Katie. "I think they want us to join them."

"No," Katie said. "That's all right."

"Come on. I can't very well dance by myself."

He led Katie on the floor, where Jack and the woman were talking animatedly. Katie reprimanded herself for feeling jealous. She knew the score. And if she couldn't deal with it, well then, she should remove herself from the lineup.

"Excuse me," Jack said. He and the woman were standing beside them. "May I cut in?"

"It's been a pleasure," Franklin said to Katie. He handed her over to Jack, who slid his arm around Katie's waist.

Franklin then leaned into the blonde and kissed her on the cheek. "Katie, meet my wife, Eloise. Eloise, this is Katie Devonworth. Katie wants everyone to know that she is not Jack's date but simply his old friend."

Jack's old friend. Ugh. He was teasing her.

As Franklin and his wife danced away, Jack looked at Katie quizzically. "What did he mean by that?" he asked as he swung her around. He took her hand and held it to his chest.

"Nothing," Katie said. Jack pulled her in closer. His blue eyes were inches away. If he leaned in any closer, their lips would touch. She swallowed and said, "He just… He thought I was your date."

"And you didn't want him to think that because you were…interested in him?"

They were moving across the floor, Jack leading and Katie doing her best to follow while concentrating on avoiding his toes. "I'm sorry to inform you," he continued, "that he and Eloise are very happy together."

"I'm not interested in him. I just didn't want him getting the wrong idea about us."

His hand clenched hers a little more tightly. "I thought you were the one who just kissed me. I thought you were the one who, not forty-eight hours ago, seduced me wearing only a sheer piece of gauze.''

Jack was closer to her now. She could see a hint of a smile on his lips. She felt the familiar stirring inside her. ''Anyway,'' he said, cheek to cheek, ''did you sing the praises of Newport Falls?''

''I tried,'' she said. ''But I'm not sure I made any difference. His mind was already made up.''

''If anyone can change Franklin's mind, it's you.''

She grinned with the praise. ''Who else do you want me to talk to tonight?''

''Just me.'' His lips brushed her head, accidental or not, and she felt a tingle all the way down to her toes.

''What about the rest of your board?''

''I'll deal with them.''

''But isn't that why I'm here?''

''No. You're here because I wanted you to talk to Franklin Bell.''

''I don't understand.''

''I know how Franklin works. If he feels anybody is trying to push a deal on him, he rejects it out of hand. I already talked to him about Newport Falls. He needed to hear about it from someone who sincerely loves it there. Franklin's a smart man. He can tell when someone is trying to work him.''

Katie was impressed that Jack had cared enough to go to the trouble to make this happen. She had asked for money for her paper. He was trying to help her save the whole community.

They danced for a moment in silence. Jack's cheek was resting against hers. She forgot about trying to follow. She let her body relax against him, allowing him to steer her across the room. The steps were formal and practiced, yet there was something inherently sensual about the way they were moving. ''When did you learn how to dance?'' she asked.

''Didn't you teach me?''

She remembered practicing with Jack before senior prom.

But it had been a couple of brief, awkward moves. She herself had no idea how to dance gracefully. But Jack made it easy. She just followed his lead. "Not like this," she said.

Jack slowed down. She could feel his warm breath against her ear. The effect was as potent as a shot of tequila.

He tightened his hold around her waist. "Katie," he said, "I want you to know that I'm very happy you're here."

She stopped dancing and looked at him. And suddenly she was tempted to kiss him again. "Well," she said, "where do we go next?"

Jack grinned. It was a devilish, rakish smile. "That's right. We do have some unfinished business to take care of."

Katie swallowed. "I was thinking about dinner."

"I forgot," Jack said, his hand brushing against her bottom. "You eat."

"What?"

"Most women I know don't eat. At least, they don't admit to it."

"Thanks again for the compliment," she joked. "You're too kind."

Jack grinned, taking her hand and leading her out of the ballroom. He helped her on with her shawl and led her to the door. Before they left, Katie pulled his arm, stopping him. "Jack," she said. "I just want to thank you again for what you're trying to do. It means more to me than you know."

He took her hand and brought it to his lips. "I want you to be happy," he said, kissing her fingers.

Katie hesitated. Jack's mouth felt so soft against her hand. So inviting. "I'm...grateful," she managed to say.

"I haven't even begun," he said. "Come on."

He led her over to where Ralph was waiting in the car. After helping her inside, he told his driver, "We have a hungry woman here, Ralph. Let's go to Fachette."

Though they drove in silence, twice Katie looked toward him. He was sitting still, his gloves in his hand, staring at her.

Katie started to feel self-conscious. Finally she asked, "Is something wrong?"

He leaned forward, and for a moment she thought he was going to kiss her. Instead he pulled the pins out of her hair. She felt a sudden sense of comfort as her hair fell to her shoulders. The only reason she had pulled it back in the first place was to try to look more elegant for him. "There," he said. "That's better."

The restaurant was crowded with people. It was dark, decorated in rich velvets and expensive-looking leather. Despite the fact that they did not have reservations, the host recognized Jack and led him immediately to a maroon velvet booth. Katie took a look at the menu and gasped. The prices were astronomical. But Jack seemed unfazed. He ordered a bottle of champagne that probably cost more than Marcella earned in a week. When it was poured, he held up a flute and made a toast. "To old friends."

Katie had the strange feeling that he was trying to prove to her that he was no longer the poor boy without a home. "You didn't have to take me here," she said. "When I said I was hungry…" She shrugged. "Hamburgers would have done."

"I know. But I thought you'd like this place."

"It's nice, definitely."

"But?"

"But it's a little stuffy. You know, uptight."

He smiled. "You prefer the diner in Newport Falls?"

"That's comparing apples with oranges." She glanced around them at the elaborately dressed couples. Everyone seemed to be tense, whispering over their menus. No one appeared to be having the kind of time the prices would merit. "It's just…I'm happy to just talk to you," she said. "To see what your life is like. I don't care where we are. Or what we eat, for that matter."

The waiter came back and Jack said, "We'd like our meals to go, please."

"To go?" the waiter asked disdainfully.

She grinned. What did Jack have up his sleeve now?

Moments later, they were walking back to the car, carrying their bags. "I have a much better place in mind," Jack said.

"Where?"

"I'd like to show you my apartment."

Katie stopped. "Your apartment?"

He nodded. "Where I live." He swung open the car door.

She said somewhat sarcastically, "Are you sure you want one of your women going there?"

"Is that what you want?" he asked, his breath against her ear. "To be one of my women?"

They looked at each other, their eyes locking. Katie felt as though he was daring her. And she had never turned down a dare. "Maybe for a night," she said, and she escaped into the car.

Jack slid in behind her. "We're going home, Ralph."

The car filled with the wonderful smell of their dinner. Within moments Ralph stopped in front of a glass high-rise that seemed to stretch into the sky. Jack held the door for Katie and she stepped out. He said hello to the doorman and they walked inside.

It looked like a grand hotel. Floral arrangements added color throughout the massive lobby, and falling water from a marble fountain echoed through the area. Jack put his hand on the narrow of her back and steered her toward the elevator.

A rush of anxiety engulfed her as the elevator doors closed. She was keenly aware of Jack standing beside her. She had dreamed of this moment many times, but never before had she imagined she might be too nervous to respond.

The elevator doors opened not onto a hallway but a large apartment. Through floor-to-ceiling windows the city, in all its glory, was lit up before them. Jack turned on the dim halogen lights that lit up a wall of art. Everything inside seemed to sparkle. Stylish black-leather-and-chrome furniture. Polished hardwood floors. It was beautiful, but it looked more like a museum than a home.

Jack put the bags down on a glass table and he pulled out a chair for her. "Shall we eat?"

Jack hadn't intended to take her back to his place. The simpler he kept things the better. Katie was not interested in a relationship with him; at least, not the kind of relationship he was interested in. So the less involved he was, the better. But he couldn't help himself around her. He wanted to be with her the way they once were. He wanted them to be friends who had their whole unblemished life in front of them.

He poured her another glass of champagne. He could already see that he had made a mistake. It was as if the real Katie had gone away. This Katie was quiet and shy. Instead of devouring her meal, she ate her steak slowly, cutting it into tiny, delicate pieces. Despite her complaint about being treated like his other women, it was quite obvious she felt uncomfortable in his home. Perhaps she, too, would've preferred to keep things simple. But if that was the case, why was she insulted by the hotel room?

"How many rooms do you have?" she asked.

"Three bedrooms, two bathrooms…this room," he said, motioning around him. "Kitchen and library," he continued. "That's it."

"What's your favorite part of the apartment?" she asked, covering her mouth so he couldn't see her chew.

"I'm hardly ever home," he said. "So I guess it would have to be the bedroom. That's the place that gets the most action." He hadn't meant for it to sound the way it did. He had just meant that most days he arrived home late at night and left first thing in the morning.

"Oh," she said, her face falling.

"I didn't mean it that way. I hardly ever…entertain here."

"Why is that?"

"Because I… Well, I don't know."

"Because you think it represents a commitment?"

"A commitment?"

"It's a personal gesture. Bringing a woman back to your home, sharing it with her."

He took a sip of his drink. Change the subject, he told himself. This conversation is going nowhere fast. But unfortunately, he said the first thing that popped into his head. "Speaking of commitments, didn't you say Matt was coming back soon?"

She shrugged. "The last I heard."

A deep, bitter feeling cut through him as his heart sank. "And how do you feel about that?" Jack forced himself to ask.

"I—" She paused. "I don't know."

Jack nodded. He saw the pain in Katie's eyes. It was enough to remind him that Matt had already laid claim to her. Regardless of her protestations, she obviously cared about her ex-husband more than she wished to admit. Jack stood up and walked over to the window.

"Jack?"

He took off his jacket and loosened his tie. Ask her if she's still in love with him, he commanded himself. Instead he said, "Well that's good news, isn't it? Maybe you two can work things out." There. He'd said it.

"What?"

Jack turned back toward her. "I told you before I want you to be happy, Katie. I meant it."

"Then stop wishing me back with Matt." Jack would've felt relief, if Katie didn't look so sad. Moments later she shook her head and said, "Did you ever think it would turn out this way?"

"What way?"

"I thought we'd all be friends for life. You, me and Matt. And now…I don't really talk to either of you."

"You're with me right now."

"Yes," she said. "But if I hadn't come to see you, would I have ever heard from you again? I don't think so. You had forgotten about me."

"Forgotten about you?" Jack couldn't believe what he was hearing. How could she possibly think he had forgotten about the only woman he had ever truly loved?

"I would never have forgotten about you, Katie. No matter how hard I tried."

"Tried?" She laughed. "Why would you try to forget about me?"

And then he knew for certain. Katie Devonworth had no idea how he felt about her. She never had. "I want you to know something. That day at the creek, when you kissed me, remember?"

She swallowed. "Uh-huh."

"It took every ounce of willpower I possessed to break away from you."

She stared at him.

"And there's not a day that's gone by since that I haven't thought about you."

Katie couldn't believe what she was hearing. This was a dream, it had to be. Jack Reilly had forgotten about her long ago.

He knelt in front of her. He cradled her head in his hands. "Not a day has gone by that I haven't wondered what would have happened between us if I had stayed." He pushed a strand of hair away from her eyes. "Do you know why I left?"

She shook her head.

"Because I knew I couldn't stop at just a kiss. I wanted you so badly, I was afraid of what was going to happen. I knew I had to stop before we'd gone too far to turn back."

"You wanted me?"

He brought her hand up to his lips and kissed it. "With all my heart," he said. He leaned forward and held both sides of her cheeks. "Do you still want me, Katie?"

She felt as if she couldn't breathe. Her heart was beating

out of control, pounding so loudly she was certain he could hear. She tried to speak but couldn't.

Jack let her go. It was obvious he had interpreted her silence as rejection. "I see," he said.

How could he doubt that she wanted him? She, who had loved him since the day she first saw him.

He attempted to stand, but she grabbed his arm and stopped him.

He turned back toward her and looked at her. She knew the moment he read the desire that was on her face. He touched her cheek with his hand and she turned toward it, kissing his fingers.

Jack leaned over and pressed his lips to hers. It was not the kiss of an amateur, but a man who knew exactly what he was doing. A man who knew how to give pleasure, as well as receive it. He kissed her softly at first, touching her lips as if savoring the taste of a fine wine. Then he cupped her face, and as his tongue slid inside her mouth, she could feel her body respond.

His hands slid inside her dress, seeking and then finding her breasts. His kisses became deeper and more intimate as he rolled her nipples in between his fingers.

He pulled back and looked into her eyes. Then, as if she was his newlywed bride, he picked her up and carried her into his bedroom.

The bedroom, like the living room, had ten-foot windows with spectacular views of the city below. "Shouldn't we shut the drapes?"

"We're miles away up here," he said. "There's no one who can see us."

He sat her down on his king-size bed and unzipped her dress. With the skill of a man who had undressed many women, he took it off. She was not wearing a bra, the dress hadn't allowed it. So Katie lay on the bed, clad only in a relatively new pair of lace panties. Usually, she felt modest and inhibited around men. With Matt, she had always turned off the light before making love. But with Jack, she welcomed the brightness from the city lights. She wanted to see him. And she wanted him to be able to see her.

She looked up at him. His white starched shirt was open at the collar, and his pressed black pants still displayed the neat pleats of the dry cleaner. How could he look so together, so in control, when she felt as if she was coming apart? "Katie," he breathed, "you are so unbelievably beautiful."

He leaned over and kissed her bare shoulder. He slid his lips to her breast, then to her nipple. She heard herself sigh and he smiled, focusing his heavy-lidded eyes on her. "I want to make you feel good," he said.

She kissed him, allowing her tongue to explore the inside of his mouth. His fingers continued to touch her, sliding underneath her panties and slowly making their way between her legs. He pushed a finger inside her and murmured, "Katie, my love."

His fingers kept working between her legs as his tongue ran a trail down her neck, her breast, then to the area below her belly button. Soon his tongue took the place of his fingers, searching, exploring, just as it had done to her mouth. She gasped and pulled him toward her, desperately yanking off his shirt and helping him to undo his pants.

She touched him, running her fingers up and down his heavy shaft. She took her time exploring, enjoying the pleasure in his eyes, till finally, she led him into her.

He surged deep inside, as if determined to claim her like no other man ever had. They continued to kiss, their tongues connected as their bodies slid back and forth. Only when she gasped and could hold back no longer did he allow himself to follow her over the edge. They clung to each other as a series of quakes rocked through them, a surge that went from his body to hers and back again.

Afterward, they lay in each other's arms, their naked bodies wrapped around each other's. Katie had thought nothing could compete with their previous lovemaking. But she was wrong.

She had never experienced such intense emotions. In fact, she had been a virgin until the age of twenty-three. Her friends had teased her about being so old and so inexperienced. But she had been waiting for Jack, hoping that she would lose her virginity with him.

When she finally did lose it, with Matt, sex was awkward, uncomfortable. Almost incestuous. It seemed inappropriate somehow to be so intimate with someone she had known and grown up with. But she had known Jack since childhood, too, and there had been none of the awkwardness. In fact, it had been just the opposite.

She could still remember the first time she and Matt made love. He had plunged into her, as if it had taken all of his nerve. Katie had responded more out of curiosity than anything else. When she'd told her mother of their awkwardness with each other, her mother had told her to be patient. "True love takes time," she'd said. "It doesn't happen overnight." And so Katie had tried, again and again. But even though they became more efficient in their lovemaking, the feeling was not there.

Not like it was with Jack.

With Jack, lovemaking was everything Katie had dreamed. Yet for some reason, she still felt a hollowness in her heart.

"Hey," he said, wrapping his arms around her, "why are you so quiet?"

"Just thinking," she said.

"About what?"

"About you, me. Us."

"Try not to think," he said. "Just feel."

But her mind was filled with thoughts. Mostly she thought of all the women who had shared their nights with Jack, of all the women who would continue to share them.

His hands moved up her leg, around her waist, and his fingers once again played with her nipples. "I'm going to make you stop thinking yet," he promised.

Whatever Jack Reilly was, he was a man of his word. Because, for that night at least, she stopped thinking and started feeling.

Jack hardly slept. He lay awake, almost afraid that if he were to sleep he would wake up and find Katie gone. Find that it had all been just a dream. A dream he had waited for almost his entire life.

He was anxious for the morning, thinking even about not going to work, of asking Katie to stay another day. He thought of the fun they could have in the city.

He smiled. This was a dramatic change for him. Even on the weekends his routine never varied. He was out the door and to his office by eight o'clock, even if he had been with a woman the night before.

Jack leaned on his side, boosting himself up so that he could get a better view of the woman sound asleep beside him. Her long lashes fluttered. A smile touched her lips. She turned toward him and snuggled in closer.

Usually he would sleep as far away from his partner as possible. But with Katie, he was content to hold her in his arms all night. He felt a warmth settle in his belly. It was more than sexual. He felt relaxed and deeply content. He wanted to stay awake, to enjoy every single minute of their time together. If he could, he would wish away the dawn, knowing that tomorrow would take her away from him once again. He wanted to stay like this, in bed with Katie in his arms, forever. He wanted to protect her from the world, to make her the happiest woman alive.

But he couldn't. For one simple reason: Katie didn't want him to. Perhaps, he thought, he could change her mind. Perhaps he could convince her that they were right for each other.

But were they? Katie would never leave Newport Falls, while he was no longer a small-town kid. His business was centered in the biggest city in the world, plus he was moving to London, where he'd be for at least two years.

He thought of himself across the Atlantic as Katie rode her

bike in the freezing cold, back toward her big, empty house. He glanced back at her, sleeping peacefully beside him. He couldn't allow that to happen. Regardless of how she felt about him, he would see that Katie's days of suffering were over. She wouldn't want for anything any longer.

Nine

By the time Katie woke, she was alone. She could hear Jack in the other room, talking quietly. She smiled as she remembered their night together. For a few precious hours, Jack had been hers once again.

But the night was over. Jack was already gone—perhaps just to the other room—and soon she would leave, return to her life alone. Agony assailed her and she pulled the sheet around her as if to ward off the pain.

She should be happy. After all, she had finally fulfilled a dream. But she couldn't help herself. She was not ready to leave Jack.

As much as a part of her wished that her feelings for him had changed, or, at the very least, he himself had changed, she still felt as intensely as she had years ago. He was her soul mate, the man she would love for the rest of her life.

But she would never have him. So why did she still cling to a hope that one day he would be hers? It was a foolish fantasy, one only made worse by their lovemaking.

She thought once again about the way he had treated her after they had made love at her house. He had been so cavalier about it, jumping up and pulling on his clothes as he instructed her to follow suit. She couldn't endure that type of treatment again, no matter how short-lived.

The only thing to do was to leave. Immediately. While she still could.

She tiptoed out of bed, reaching for her dress on the chair. When she found her panties on the floor she slipped them on. Jack opened the door just as she was about to step into her dress. She yanked it up and held it in place with her hands.

"Good morning," he said. He was wearing a white robe. His hair was tousled but he was clean-shaven. "I was on the phone with my office."

"Oh," she said, trying not to look at him.

He crossed his arms and said, "Eager to leave?"

She shrugged. "I, uh, should get going."

"Okay."

She didn't budge.

"Did you want to borrow some sweats?"

"I don't care," she said as casually as she could manage.

"Okay," he said. He opened up his closet and handed her a sweatshirt. She realized he was waiting for her to take it from him, which would mean, as they both knew, her dress would fall. She reached out her hand, but he grabbed it before she got to the shirt. Within a second she was flat on her back again, lying on the bed.

He leaned over her. "That was a basic move, Devonworth. The champagne must've fogged your brain." He began kissing her neck. "I'm reneging on my promise."

"What promise?"

"The just-one-night promise."

"You are?"

His hands were on her body again, touching her breasts. She could feel her body respond in spite of her mind. Leave, she commanded herself. Now! But her body had turned to jelly. "I was hoping," he began, "we could take the day off and spend some time...getting acquainted."

"I thought we already did that," she said.

His hand slipped down under the sheets, his fingers taking down her panties and touching her most sensitive, private part. "I'd like to show you the city, Katie. Take you to the theater and out to dinner...someplace that's not as stuffy as the one I took you to last night. Tomorrow I'll let you return to your beloved Newport Falls."

Katie's mind went blank. She couldn't think. She could only feel. And what she was feeling was heavenly. "How can you do that?" she said on a sigh.

"Do what?" he asked, his fingers rubbing her to distraction.

"Talk to me while you touch me like that." She inhaled sharply as his finger went inside her.

"Like that?" he said. "Or like this?" One finger was inside her, the other circling around and around.

His lips were curled into a sexy grin as he leaned over, obviously enjoying her mounting haze of ecstasy. "You seem a little distracted. But I really need an answer now, otherwise I have to go to the office—"

Before he could finish, she kissed him. Reaching under his robe, she had no trouble locating his hard, erect shaft. She ran her fingers up and down, caressing him. "What's wrong?" she murmured. "You seem a little distracted yourself."

He answered her by taking her in his arms and sliding inside her. Holding her arms down against the bed, he moved back and forth, careful to brush her in all the right places.

"Look at me," he whispered.

She opened her eyes to the sun-filled room. It seemed too intimate, so uninhibited to be staring into his eyes as he pushed himself deeper and deeper inside her. Jack kept going, changing his speed and pressure, till finally Katie couldn't hold back any longer. She arched her back, holding on to his hands for dear life. When relief came, it was an eruption so intense, she could swear the very earth had moved. And at the same time, his body shuddered and he closed his eyes. A smile crossed his lips.

He kissed her forehead and lay down beside her. He took her in his arms. "So? Are we on for lunch?"

She laughed. "Typical guy. One-track mind."

He boosted himself up on one arm and leaned over her. He ran his finger around her mouth. "Mine's one-track. It's only focused on you. Stay today, Katie. Let me show you my town."

"I have to call my office," she said.

He smiled. "I'll be in the shower."

He stood up, his lean body unfolding in front of her. She held the pillow against her chest as she admired his broad, strong shoulders and his tight, muscular butt. He still had the body of an athlete.

He appeared to have lost all modesty, walking around naked as if it was the most natural thing in the world. He tossed her his robe before he left.

As the shower ran, she threw on the robe and called Marcella. She was careful not to reveal that she was in Jack's apartment, instead of his corporate offices. As she was talking on the phone, she glanced around Jack's pristine, almost sterile-looking contemporary bedroom. It had the feel of a plush hotel room. White bed, white walls, all framed by a spectacular view of the city. There was no sense of home in this room, no sense of the owner or what he was like. Except...

She hung up the phone and walked over to a framed picture on the wall. It was the three of them: earth, wind and fire. It was taken when they were in the fifth grade. Matt was leaning forward, his face resting in his hands. Jack was looking to the side, as if eager to escape. Katie had her arms around both boys, but her eyes and face were focused on Jack.

"Remember that picture?" Jack asked. He had appeared behind her, a towel wrapped around his waist.

"Sure," Katie said. Although she wasn't sure if she remembered that exact picture. There were many pictures taken throughout their childhood, pictures from camping trips, school plays, high-school dances. But she wasn't sure they had captured the spirit of the three as well as this one. Matt's aloofness, Jack's ache to escape, and her love for Jack.

"It was taken the day we started fifth grade."

"Of course," she said.

"Why don't you get dressed?" Jack said. "We have to stop at my office for a few minutes and then I'm all yours."

The heavens had seen fit to give her one more day with him, and she intended to make the most of it. She picked up her blue chiffon dress. "Do you think it's formal enough for Reilly Investments?"

He laughed. "There's a flexible dress code, but unfortunately we don't allow chiffon."

"What about bathrobes?"

"Only if you're naked underneath." He winked. "I took the liberty of having your things sent over here from the hotel."

"You took the liberty? When?"

"Early this morning. Before you woke." He walked into the other room and brought back her suitcase. "Here you go, Lois Lane."

She was glad that she didn't have to schlep all the way to the hotel. This type of luxury, of having things just taken care of for her, might be new, but she could get used to it quickly.

She pulled her red suit out of her suitcase and shook out the wrinkles. She got dressed quickly in a white turtleneck, the suit and black heels. She'd worn this outfit so many times before, she didn't bother looking in the mirror. She may not win any fashion awards, but this was the best she could do. After all, she had never been a clotheshorse.

But for once, she sort of wished she was. She felt a little funny next to Jack, with his expensive designer suit made just for him and his Italian leather shoes.

"What's wrong?" Jack asked a half hour later as they

headed into his office. His demeanor had changed from the moment they set foot in his building. His pace quickened and his brow tightened. It was as if he had transformed back into Jack the entrepreneur, the tough guy who didn't let anyone or anything get in his way.

"Nothing," she said.

He led her into the waiting room. The receptionist straightened as he approached. The coy smile she gave Jack as he passed made Katie feel a pang of possessiveness toward him. She straightened her suit and followed him through another set of double doors.

Jack's assistant, an efficient-looking woman in her mid-forties, jumped to attention. She looked surprised when she saw Katie.

"Janice," Jack said, as he brushed past her, "you remember Katie Devonworth."

"Of course. How are you, Ms. Devonworth?"

"Fine," Katie said. "Nice to see you again."

"Jack," Janice said, following him into his office. "I canceled everything as you requested. But what did you want to do about the trade cocktail party tonight?"

Jack stopped. "I forgot about that." He looked at Katie.

"If you have to go, I understand," Katie began.

Still looking at Katie, he asked his assistant, "Is Howard Berman attending?"

"He's supposed to."

Katie asked, "Howard Berman of Berman's department store?"

Jack nodded, thinking. He turned back toward Janice and said, "Call and tell them I'll be bringing a guest."

"I'll take care of it," she said, looking at Katie once again before she left.

"What would you like for lunch?" Jack asked as the door closed. "There's a wonderful French re—"

"A cheeseburger," Katie said. "I'm so hungry I could eat a horse." After a night of rambunctious lovemaking, and a morning of the same, she was famished. Only good old American food would fit the bill.

"Me, too," Jack said with a smile. "I know just the place."

An hour later they were in Midtown, eating the best burgers Katie had ever tasted. The restaurant was exactly what she'd hoped for—big and loud, with lots of distractions. Ever since she and Jack had arrived at his office, they'd both been quiet. Katie had busied herself by focusing on her surroundings, both in the office while he worked and here at the restaurant.

As they left the restaurant, Jack took her hand. It was a beautiful winter day with a bright sun that warmed them as they walked. Jack led her to Fifth Avenue, where they admired the displays in the store windows. "Do you want to go inside?" Jack asked as she stared at the Saks display.

She shook her head. "I'm a much better window-shopper."

She started walking again, but Jack pulled her to a stop. "You don't like New York, do you?"

"Sure, I like it. I don't know if I'd want to live here, but it's fun to visit."

He grabbed her hands and gently nudged her against the building. He leaned into her, pressing up against her. His breath grew shallow and she could feel the hardness inside his pants.

"But if you lived in a big city," Jack said softly, "think of how much fun you could have."

"Fun?" she asked. So that was all she meant to him. Fun.

She pushed him back and said, "I have responsibilities in Newport Falls. I have people who count on me. New York, at least the New York you've shown me, is a pretty place, but I have a home in Newport Falls, not to mention a business and—"

"Calm down, Katie," he said. "No one is asking you to leave Newport Falls. I was just saying that it's nice having you here. With me." He took her hand. "That's all."

He paused a beat, staring at her, as if trying to read her.

Then he checked his watch. "Come on," he said, taking her arm. They walked a couple of blocks to where Ralph was waiting.

He helped her into the car. "Where are we going?" she asked.

"Still like dinosaurs?"

As a child, she had always had a knack for science. She was fascinated with anything from the prehistoric age, including dinosaurs. "Who doesn't?" she asked.

Jack laughed. "Ralph," he said, "will you please take us to the Museum of Natural History?"

It had been a long time since Katie had wandered around a museum. She and Jack strolled around, hand in hand, as if they had all the time in the world. Afterward, Jack led her back out to where Ralph was waiting. As she slipped inside the warm car, she asked, "Where next?"

Jack glanced at his watch. "It's almost time for our stuffy cocktail party," he said.

"If it's so stuffy, why are we going?"

He leaned forward. "I think you've already guessed the answer to that. Newport Falls needs another department store. And your paper needs advertising revenues."

"So Berman is looking to expand?"

"I'm hoping you'll convince him."

Although Jack's faith in her was flattering, she wondered how in the world she could convince the owner of one of the largest department store chains to open a branch in Newport Falls.

But as they drove to the meeting, Jack calmed her with advice that made her task seem simple: be natural and talk about Newport Falls as much as possible.

They walked into the crowded Oak Room on the first floor of the Plaza. She stood back as Jack greeted the people around him. He was so confident, self-assured. And why wouldn't he be? The small-town boy had shed his insecurities long ago.

When Jack pulled her into the group, she followed his lead,

talking to the people he seemed most interested in. When he left to get drinks, a tall, attractive brunette walked up to her and stuck out her hand. "You must be Katie Devonworth," she said.

"Yes." Katie nodded, surprised that someone there already knew who she was.

"I'm Susan Miller from Yacobi Investments. Jack and I go way back. He told me about your paper."

"Great," Katie said. Was Susan a potential investor?

"I'm sorry to hear things aren't going well. Do you think you'll move to New York when it folds?"

The woman couldn't have delivered more force if she had hit Katie between the eyes. "Folds?" Katie asked. "It's not folding."

"Oh," she said. "I thought Jack said… Well, never mind. So you're staying put, then? In Newport Springs?"

"Newport *Falls*."

"Newport Falls," she said, thinking. "Newport Falls… My parents have a country house in Vermont. I know we've passed the exit for Newport Falls a million times, but I just can't place exactly where it is."

Katie glanced around for Jack. Where was he? And what had he said to this woman that would make her think the paper was about to fold?

"Anyway," Susan continued, "I'm sure you're not too happy about Jack. I tried to talk him out of it myself." She laughed. It was a cold, bitter sound. "But that didn't seem to make much difference. Perhaps you'll have more luck."

Katie felt someone brush up against her. It was Jack. He said, "I see you've met Susan."

"Jack," Susan said. She took his hand and leaned over, kissing his cheek. Then she motioned toward Katie. "What a lovely friend you have here."

"Thank you, Susan." He looked amused, as if aware that Susan was playing some sort of game. "Now, if you'll excuse us, I want to introduce my friend to Mr. Berman." Jack led

Katie across the room and introduced her to a short, squat man. Within moments, Jack had steered the conversation to Newport Falls. Katie followed his lead, raving about the benefits of having a business there.

Several times she saw Jack look at her and wink, encouraging her to continue. But Mr. Berman did not look impressed. In fact, he didn't even appear to be listening. More than once she caught him looking over her shoulder, as if waiting to be rescued. In the end, she doubted her performance had made any difference.

After the party, they retrieved their coats. Jack was helping her put hers on when he grabbed her around the waist and kissed her neck. "Where would you like to go next?"

She shrugged and stepped away from him. "Berman wasn't interested, was he?"

"Maybe not, but he's not the only possibility out there."

"Jack," she said, grabbing both his hands. "I appreciate what you're trying to do for me, and for the town. I do. But I think I'm out of my league here. I don't know anything about how to entice businesses to—"

"But I do. And I'm helping you." Jack held the door open for Katie. As Katie walked beside him, she brushed against his chest. Jack smiled at her as if she had intentionally teased him.

Katie stepped outside. A blast of wintry air caused her to pause. "I'm a newspaperwoman. It's the only thing I know."

"You sell yourself short, Katie. You could do a lot of things. You will, if you have to."

"You mean if *The Falls* fails."

He squeezed her hand as they walked down the street. "We're going to make sure that doesn't happen," he assured her.

"Susan Miller seems to think that *The Falls* is going down the tubes."

"I'm surprised she knows anything about it."

"She said you told her about it."

He met her eyes directly. "I would never discuss *The Falls* with Susan, or anything else for that matter. I barely know her."

"She seemed to know me."

"She's friends with Franklin. Maybe he said something to her about you. But I can't imagine he knows anything about your paper or your financial situation." He pulled her to a stop and swung her into him. He paused, still looking at her. "But that's not what's bothering you, is it?"

She hesitated, then blurted out, "I just...I guess I just feel a little strange about this. About us."

"Oh," Jack said. His mouth tightened into a grimace. He let go of her hands and began walking again. "The last thing I want is to make you uncomfortable. I thought that, well, last night was what you wanted."

"It was."

"So what's wrong?" He had stopped again. His hands were in his pocket.

What's wrong was that she needed more. A declaration of undying love. A promise that he would never, ever touch another woman. That he would never even be tempted.

But that was ridiculous. Because they were two old friends who, until recently, hadn't spoken in years. They were business acquaintances who had shared a night of passion.

And if she wasn't careful, it would be their one and only. She glanced down at the ground. "Nothing," she said. "I think the sex part has me a little confused. I don't often sleep with my...friends."

"What about your business associates?" he asked.

She knew he was joking. But, considering the circumstances, she didn't find him funny. She turned to face him. "Have you ever slept with Susan?"

"What?" he asked. "Susan who?"

"Susan from the party."

"No," he said. "What would give you that idea?"

Katie thought again about what Susan had said. *I'm sure you're not too happy about Jack...*

"She was saying some strange things, as if she was certain I wasn't too happy with you."

"Are you?" he asked quietly.

"Am I what?"

Jack put his arm around her and pulled her close. "Happy with me?"

Yes, Katie wanted to say. But then again, what woman wouldn't be? He was kind, smart, sexy....

But he was not hers.

"Of course," she said. "You've been a big help to me."

"Is that all?" he asked. She looked up at him. He held her arms against her sides. He seemed almost desperate...for the truth.

But the truth, she knew, was something that would send him running in the other direction. And she was not ready to say goodbye. "We're friends," she said.

Friends. He was beginning to despise the word. Yet Katie couldn't seem to help hammering it in. She obviously suspected what he was feeling and was doing her best to remind him she did not return his affection.

He had hoped their night together would have helped change her mind. But it hadn't. The old Katie, he knew, could never separate sex from love. But Katie had been hardened by life. The new version seemed more than willing to distinguish between the two.

"What's wrong?" she asked. "Did I say something?"

No, Jack thought. It was not what she said. It was what she felt—or didn't feel—that upset him. "Let's go," he said. He led her over to where Ralph was waiting with the car. Katie climbed in, settling against the window as if afraid Jack might grab her and start professing his love. Jack stayed on his side and crossed his arms. Fortunately, his cell phone rescued him. He pulled it out and snapped it open.

"Jack?" It was Carol Casey.

"Yes?" He could tell from the tone of her voice that something was wrong.

"What the hell is going on? Howard Berman just called me. He was so excited, I thought he was going to have an accident. Did you tell him you were interested in buying him out?"

Not in so many words. He had hoped that Howard might be interested in opening up a branch of Berman's himself. But Howard wasn't interested in opening up a new store. In fact, he was looking to retire from his business completely. So when Katie left for the ladies' room, Jack had made Berman a loose offer.

Normally Jack would have had no interest in buying a department store chain. He specialized in high tech, not retail. But in this case he was interested. And it was because of Franklin Bell.

Jack had spoken to him that morning. Franklin was taking a second look at Newport Falls, but although he agreed that the savings for his company would be impressive, he was still discouraged. How could he convince his employees to move to a place so isolated that the closest shopping center was nearly an hour away? Besides that, it felt like a town on the brink of death.

So Jack had asked how he would feel if he personally guaranteed new business in town. That wasn't enough for Franklin. He wanted a major department store.

Berman's fit the bill.

He told Carol none of this, simply said, "If there's no other way." He glanced at Katie. She had opened up her phone and was checking her messages.

"Jack," Carol warned, "how do you plan on financing this? Everything is tied up in our European venture."

"We'll have to make it work," Jack said.

"I can't get blood from turnips."

Jack glanced at Katie. She had put away her phone and was looking at him.

"If anyone can, it's you," Jack told Carol.

"Berman wants to meet with you tomorrow at noon. He wants a written offer."

"Then we need to give him one," Jack said, snapping his phone shut.

"Problem at the office?" Katie asked.

"Not really."

"If you have to go back in, I understand. You've spent a lot of time with me today. I hope I haven't been too much of an imposition."

She was talking like a peer, not like a woman with whom he had spent hours making love.

Perhaps she wanted to forget about their previous night. Perhaps she wanted a fresh start. But that, Jack swore, was not going to happen. Within a split second he had pulled Katie close to him.

His lips brushed her ear. He touched her silky hair as he reveled in her soft scent. Desire surged though him. He would have liked nothing better than to close the driver partition and take her right there in the back of the limousine.

But the car had stopped. They were at Jack's apartment building. "Thanks, Ralph," Jack said. He let go of Katie and picked up his briefcase. "Have a good night."

Katie and Jack walked through the lobby, neither speaking nor touching. Katie welcomed the silence, so flushed was she from the interaction in the car. Jack's touch was enough to make her abandon any pretense of the chaste friendship she was so desperately claiming.

They stepped into the elevator. As they left the ground behind, Katie stared at the numbers above the door, watching the floors fly past. Out of the corner of her eye, she saw Jack. He was staring at her, his mouth set in grim resolve. "What?" she asked.

But he didn't answer.

The doors opened and Katie stepped out. "If I said something wrong—"

But she didn't have time to finish. Jack had his arms wrapped around her, his fingers on her mouth. "No more talking," he whispered. He began kissing the back of her neck as he undid the buttons on her blouse.

Without missing a beat, he steered her back toward the couch. As he undid the last button, her legs bumped up against the sofa. Jack Reilly, she realized, was one smooth operator. She couldn't help but wonder how many women had experienced this walk of seduction.

But it didn't matter, she told herself. Jack Reilly belonged to her for one more night.

He didn't bother to remove either her blouse or her jacket. In one skilled move he pushed up her bra while his other hand unclasped it. He leaned before her, taking her nipples in his mouth. Katie felt her body melt into him as her mind went blank. She ran her fingers through his soft, thick hair. Jack kissed her belly, holding her to him as he kissed her legs through her skirt. He reached underneath it and massaged the top of her legs. Then he lifted up her skirt and ran his tongue over her stocking, riding up as far as her inner thigh, while the other hand removed her shoes.

Katie couldn't move. The passion stunned her, the feeling building inside her a train gaining speed.

Jack paused, taking just enough time to remove his tie. Then he kissed her belly as he undid the button on her skirt. He hooked his fingers inside her hose and pulled them both off with one swoop. With one arm he lifted her up, and with the other, he removed the remainder of her clothes.

And then he smiled. "You are so beautiful," he said.

Katie lay on the leather couch, totally naked in front of him. The rich scent of the leather along with its sleek feel only added to the eroticism.

He ran his index finger around the corner of her eye. "Close your eyes," he instructed.

Katie followed his directive, closing her eyes tightly.

"Tell me what you feel," he said.

She reached out and blindly touched Jack's face. She ran her fingers across his five-o'clock stubble and felt for his lips. He kissed them, taking them into his mouth and sucking on them gently. Then she ran them across his beautiful eyes, over his heavy lashes and around the circumference of his face. She worked slowly, committing this beautiful moment to memory. Her hands slid down to his neck and she met his crisply starched shirt. She ran her fingers over his muscled back and arms until her hands settled on his waist.

"Keep going," she heard him say.

She slid down the couch and ran her fingers over his belt and down the front of his Armani slacks. She felt his hardness and pulled him toward her. She arched forward, pushing her hips up against him.

"I feel you," she said. "You want me."

"Not yet." He took her hands away from him and held them over her head. She felt his tongue on her breast, sucking and circling. Then he slid lower, his fingers massaging her naked flesh as they went. He spread her legs and moved between them, his fingers circling around her pleats of flesh, sliding up and over her. "What are you feeling?" he whispered.

"You," she managed to say. She grabbed on to the armrest of the couch, digging her fingernails into the leather. "You make me feel wonderful."

His tongue slipped inside her and then back up through her soft pleats and over her pointed ridge. He did this over and over, up and down and back inside. She lost all sense of time and meaning. All she cared about was the physical, the touch of Jack's lips as they grazed her inner thigh, exploring and searching.

The pressure began to surge, but she knew she could not let go. Not yet. "Take me, Jack," she said. "Now."

She opened her eyes and reached for his buckle. But he was already ahead of her. He had unzipped his pants. She reached inside. Jack was big and hard, his swollen shaft as finely toned as the rest of his body. As she touched him he arched his back and gasped with pleasure. She led him toward her, raising her hips to greet him. As he slipped inside her dark wetness, she felt her body explode with heat. She drove herself against him, her body taking over her mind. She was no longer Katie, the prim girl from Newport Falls. The ice princess had melted. Katie now cared about one thing: satisfaction.

Jack moved up and down, his eyes never leaving hers. Like an expert skilled in seduction, he read the signals, knowing exactly when to speed up or slow down. He knew how to move to create the friction that drove her wild. "Tell me when," he said as his body grew rigid. Release was imminent.

She could feel it building, building, "Now," she cried.

Jack groaned. His muscles tightened, fighting against the inevitable. Suddenly he shuddered. As his warm seed spilled into her she felt surge after surge of a pleasure unlike anything she had ever experienced.

Afterward they both lay without moving, cheek to cheek, heart to heart. Finally Jack lifted himself up with one arm. He leaned over her and touched the upper part of her breast.

"You still have your clothes on," she said.

He glanced down at himself and smiled. "You're right. I guess someone was working a little too slowly." He sat up and ran his fingers through his hair. "Can I get you anything? Something to drink or eat…"

"I'll take a robe," she said. She was overcome by the urge to cover herself. With Jack no longer on top of her, she suddenly felt extremely vulnerable and exposed.

He came back carrying the same white terry-cloth robe she

had worn that morning. He sat down next to her and kissed her shoulders before slipping it across them.

Suddenly Katie said quietly, "Jack? Do you ever think about what might have happened between us if you hadn't walked away that day at the creek?"

Jack's smiled faded, and once again, Katie regretted bringing up the past.

"I try not to" was all he said.

Of course, thought Katie. She clutched the robe to her and stood. She walked over to the window and touched the cold glass.

"Katie," he said, "what is it? What did I say?"

She turned back to him. And once again she felt the feeling that had haunted her most of her life. She loved Jack and only Jack. And she always would.

As with the night before, Jack stayed awake long after Katie had fallen asleep. Two nights in a row without sleep, yet he felt strangely exhilarated.

The return of Katie had thrown him a curveball he had not been expecting. He thought he'd known exactly where he was going. He was on his way to becoming one of the most powerful businessmen in the world. But the business to which he had devoted his life paled in comparison to his feelings for Katie. He would've gladly traded it all to have been with her.

It was apparent, however, that Katie did not share his sentiment. Still, he owed her the truth. Katie Devonworth was the only woman he loved. The only woman he would ever love.

She deserved to know that he would continue to do everything in his power to guarantee her happiness.

And if she didn't want him? If she didn't feel the same way? If she didn't think she could ever feel the same way?

That was a chance he was willing to take.

Jack must've fallen asleep because when he opened his eyes, the moon had set and the sun's brightness permeated the room. He smiled as he reached out for Katie.

But she wasn't there.

"Katie?" Her name was met with silence.

He threw the covers off and jumped out of bed. "Katie?" he called out again.

There, on his dressing table, was a note written in her handwriting.

Jack,

I thought we'd avoid any awkward goodbyes. Thank you again for your help.

Love,
Katie

His heart sagged in disappointment, disappointment almost immediately replaced by anger. Blood pumped through his veins as his heart accelerated. So this was it? This was to be her goodbye?

No! He had just gotten her back. There was no way in hell he was going to let her say goodbye like this. If this was to be the end, she would have to say goodbye to his face.

He grabbed his clothes. He was going to Newport Falls.

Ten

The sun had been in the sky for exactly two hours by the time Katie's train arrived in Newport Falls. As she pulled her carry-on out of the small station, the night before came floating back in visual clips. Jack, his fingers, his nakedness.

She climbed into a taxi and gave the driver directions to her home. She caught her reflection in the driver's rearview mirror. She looked as tousled and disheveled as she felt. Such was her hurry to leave Jack's that she hadn't bothered to shower or even brush her hair. She was afraid the slightest noise would wake him.

She hadn't intended for their time to end with her sneaking out of his apartment like a common thief. But this morning she woke up cuddled against him, her arms wrapped around his neck. As she listened to his calm, steady breath, she felt a love so pure and real, she knew nothing would ever compare.

The only thing to do was to leave. Immediately. While she still could.

Ugh! She hated feeling like this. Before Jack had reappeared in her life she had been content. Perhaps it had not been the life she had hoped, but she had grown accustomed to it. There may not have been the intense highs that come with love, but she didn't have to endure the lows, either.

But these few days with Jack had sent her into a tailspin. How could she ever return to a life without him?

But she would. Because she had to. Katie had never been able to tolerate people who refused to take responsibility for their actions. She realized that she and she alone was responsible for her predicament. She knew getting involved with the man she had loved so intensely was risky. After all, she knew Jack inside and out. He would never live in Newport Falls. Nor would he ever consent to a life with her. She knew that from the beginning. But she had not only chosen to open her heart to him again, she had slept with him.

She pressed her warm cheek against the cool window and watched the world pass by. A fresh dusting of snow had coated the woods and fields along the highway. Everything appeared calm and peaceful.

The cab had no trouble making it up her long driveway. She couldn't help but notice the fresh plow marks. Thank goodness, she thought. She didn't feel like trudging up the drive with her bag.

She paid the cabbie and made her way up the steps and opened the door. She stepped inside and turned on the light. She immediately sensed she was not alone.

Alarmed, she took a step backward. But she wasn't fast enough. The door slammed shut.

"Where have you been?"

Matt was standing beside her.

"Matt," she breathed. She dropped her suitcase. "You scared me." She had not seen her ex-husband in two years. His time away had changed him. Despite his bronzed skin, he looked sickly. He was thinner than she had ever seen him and his hair was long and scraggy. He was wearing jeans and an old flannel shirt that she recognized as having belonged to her dad. "What are you doing here?" she asked, too startled to welcome him.

"Where have you been?" he repeated.

"In New York," she said. "And answer my question. What are you doing here?"

"I got in last night," Matt said, taking her carry-on bag and placing it out of the way.

"So you came here?"

"Of course," Matt said, without skipping a beat.

"I didn't see your car."

"I parked in the garage," he said. "Like I always do."

Katie turned to him, stunned. Like he always did? He had been gone for two years. They were divorced.

"What were you doing in New York?" he asked.

This was strange. Too strange. Matt was acting as if their relationship had suffered a mere hiccup. As if he had been gone two days instead of two years. "I had a business meeting," Katie said.

Matt looked at her. He squinted and crossed his arms. "What kind of business?"

But Katie could tell by the way Matt was acting that he knew exactly where she had gone and whom she had seen. "What do you want, Matt?"

At the tone of her voice, his expression lightened. He kissed her on the cheek. "It's good to see you, Katie," he said. He tried to take her hand but she shook him off. "Hey," he said. "Relax. I'm not here to give you the third degree. I just stopped by to say hello."

"But I wasn't here. So you let yourself into my house?"

"It was my house, too," Matt said. He brushed a piece of hair away from her face.

The loving gesture made Katie cringe. She wanted to slap his hand away. "This has not been your house in years," Katie said. "You should've called."

"I did. And when you didn't answer, I got concerned. I came over to check up on you."

"I've managed fine in the past two years."

"That makes one of us," he said. He slunk past her, heading into the living room.

It was as if she was watching a balloon deflate. His cockiness seemed to fade away with the admission of regret. She reminded herself that he had initiated the divorce, but still, his confession stirred her pity.

Katie followed him into the living room. Matt was sitting on the couch, his head in his hands. She crossed her arms and said, "We can talk later. Right now you need to leave. I have to get ready for work."

"How is he?" Matt asked, picking up his head and looking into the fire he'd made.

Katie knew he was referring to Jack. She had no doubt the entire town knew exactly where she had spent the last two nights. Still, a direct question deserved a direct answer. "He's doing great."

Matt nodded. "I always knew this would happen sooner or later."

"Knew what would happen?"

"What do you think?"

Suddenly, she saw Matt at the creek all those years ago. *I know you love him,* he had said. *I've known for a long time. Everyone has.* Katie shook her head. "He's lending me money," she said.

Matt laughed. It was a strange, hollow sound. "Oh, I see. It's just business."

"More or less."

Matt nodded slowly. She didn't care if he believed her or not. It was the truth, as much as she might wish otherwise.

Matt said, "I heard *The Falls* is in trouble." He looked suspicious, as if he didn't quite believe the rumors.

"Everything in Newport Falls is in trouble," Katie replied defensively.

"So how much is Jack going to give you? A million? Two million? Or nothing at all?"

"That is none of your business."

Matt looked at her and said, "He hasn't agreed to invest anything, has he?"

Katie remained steady. "I think you should go."

"Are you familiar with the term *due diligence?*"

"It's time to go, Matt," she repeated.

But Matt continued on. "It means the board members have to agree on an investment first. That investment needs to show signs of growth, needs to be lucrative. The board at Reilly Investments would never approve of *The Falls.*"

"That's not true." Katie thought back to what Susan Miller had said. *When it folds…*

"The board of any company would never approve a loan to your paper and you know it," Matt said. "That's why you went to him in the first place. Hell, everyone in town knows it, Katie."

"He's offered his help…."

"It's all bullshit, Katie. Just to get you in the sack. Did he fly you to New York on his private jet? He likes to fly his women on his jet."

"That's enough," Katie said.

But Matt kept going. "He was playing you, Katie, playing you to get back at me. He's always been jealous of me, always wanted whatever I had. He never had any interest in you until he found I had asked you to marry me. That's the only time he—"

"You have no right!" Katie interrupted. "No right to come here and make accusations! You left with another woman. Two years ago."

"I'm flattered you even noticed."

"You were my husband!"

"In title only. We both know you never loved me."

"You're wrong, Matt," she said. "I cared about you very much."

"But it didn't compare to what you felt for Jack, did it?" He paused and then said, "What you still feel."

Katie was silent for a moment. Then she said, "Why did you come back?"

Matt looked at her. "I needed to see you. To stop you from making a mistake."

"A mistake?"

He shifted his eyes. "Jack can't give you what you want."

"Matt," Katie said. She sighed and her expression softened. "We both know it's over between us. It has nothing to do with Jack. We never should've been together in the first place."

"It has everything to do with Jack. Everything to do with your ridiculous fantasy about sharing your life with him. Let's not forget that he left you, Katie. He left. I was the one who stayed by your side day after day, hour after hour. While Jack was squiring around some of the most beautiful girls in Europe, I was the one helping you with your mother. I was the one who stayed."

You eventually left, too, Katie wanted to remind him.

"You think this time is different, don't you?" Matt continued. "Why? Because you finally slept together?" Matt laughed again. "You don't get it, do you? Jack Reilly sleeps with anyone and everyone these days. Even old friends."

"I'm not naive," Katie said. "And I don't need you to protect me."

"Really? Then you won't need my shoulder to cry on when Jack moves to London."

Katie's face fell. Jack was leaving?

"You didn't know, did you?" Matt said, grabbing her wrist.

No. Matt was lying. He had to be.

"It was in yesterday's *Wall Street Journal*," he continued. "Reilly Investments is opening up a branch in London, headed up personally by Jack Reilly himself."

Jack was leaving...Jack was leaving....

But what difference did it make? After all, hadn't she

known all along that their romance would be short-lived? Isn't that why she left without saying goodbye, because she knew a goodbye was inevitable?

"I guess you're stuck with me once again," Matt said.

"It's over, Matt. We're divorced." Katie tried to pull away, but Matt just dug his fingers in deeper. "Let me go," she said. "You're hurting me."

"You're such a fool," Matt said. "Don't you get it?"

"Let go of her!" Jack was standing in the doorway. Neither had heard him come in.

Surprised, Matt dropped Katie's wrist.

Jack? she thought. Jack was here? Her mind started spinning at the sight of him.

"How perfect," Matt said. "Prince Charming has arrived in search of Cinderella. Did she leave a shoe when she left this morning—"

Before he could finish, Jack's fist made contact with his nose. Matt fell to the ground.

"Keep your hands off her," Jack growled.

"She's my wife!"

"Not anymore." Jack grabbed him by the lapels and lifted him up. "How could you do that to her, Matt? You promised me you would take care of her... Instead you hurt her!"

"No worse than you," Matt said, attempting a swing. But Jack caught his arm and tossed it away.

"Stop it, please," Katie said. She felt as if she was having a bad dream. Matt and Jack...both together. Fighting.

Jack hesitated. Reluctantly, he set Matt down.

"Jack," Katie said, "what are you doing here?"

"I..." He paused as he looked at her. "You left before I could tell you... Well, before I could tell you how I feel."

"We already know how you feel." Matt smirked.

Jack turned toward him, and Matt shrank back.

"Matt," Katie said, "I think you should go."

"He can hear this," Jack said. "He's heard it before." He

took a step toward her and stopped. "I love you, Katie. I always have."

Katie wasn't sure she had heard him correctly. He loved her? Jack loved her?

"Haven't I, Matt?" Jack asked.

Matt laughed. "That's right. You loved her so much you left her the first chance you had. You loved her when you left for college. You loved her when you never returned, not even for summer breaks. You loved her when you accepted that position in Europe right after her dad died.... You're right, Jack. I guess nothing's changed."

"Stop it, Matt," Katie said quietly. She opened the door. "Please leave. Now!"

Matt gave them both a rough salute and walked to the door. He stopped there and said, "Congratulations, Jack. I guess you win. But there was never much of a competition, was there?" He looked at Katie. "I'm gone. Just remember, sometimes love isn't enough." He shrugged. "After all, I should know."

Katie closed the door after him. "I'm sorry, Katie," Jack said. "I'm sorry you had to go through that." He made a move toward her, but Katie retreated. She knew if he touched her, just once, she would lose whatever mind power she still had. And she needed a clear head to think. To process what had just happened.

"Are you all right?" he asked.

She nodded. "I'm sorry I left like I did this morning. I don't like goodbyes."

"So let's not say it."

She thought about what Matt had said. Was Jack moving to Europe?

"Hey," Jack said softly. He was standing in front of her. He cupped her chin and tilted her head toward him.

As she looked into his eyes, her doubt faded.

She turned her head away. What difference did it make? He loved her. He loved her. But as much as she reminded herself, she could not believe it. She didn't want to admit it but she agreed with Matt. If Jack truly loved her, could he have left her the way he did?

"Look at me, Katie," he said. "Look at me and tell me you're ready to say goodbye."

With his free hand, he began stroking her arm. "You shouldn't have left," Jack said quietly.

"I didn't think it made any difference," she said. "I was leaving this morning, anyway."

"Maybe not."

"I have to go to work," Katie said weakly.

"You're in a meeting," Jack said, kissing her neck. "A meeting with a very important investor."

Katie felt as if she was about to pass out. Matt, Jack… It was too much. *I love you,* he had said. *I love you….*

Katie broke away. "You shouldn't have come here, Jack. It's just prolonging the inevitable."

"The inevitable?" Jack asked. "But it doesn't have to be that way."

Her willpower was beginning to fade. She couldn't stand there a minute longer or she would be taking off her clothes and jumping back in his arms. "I have to go," she said. She ran upstairs and stepped into the bathroom, where she started the shower. Sitting down on the side of the tub, she breathed deeply. It had taken all of her strength to break away from Jack.

She stripped down and stepped into the shower. The frigid water pelted her body, and for once she welcomed the chill. She scrubbed her skin, as if trying to wash away Matt's words. She thought about what he had said regarding due diligence. She didn't believe it. After all, Jack was doing everything he could to help her. He would've told her point-blank if he couldn't get her the money.

And about him moving to Europe again… Her heart sank at the thought of it. But why should she be surprised? Matt

vas right. Love was not enough to keep Jack in Newport
Falls.

She turned off the shower and towel-dried her hair. Then
she wrapped the towel around her and peeked out. The hall
was empty. She hurried into her bedroom, shutting the door
behind her. When she turned around, she jumped. Jack was
sitting on her bed, waiting for her.

"What's going on?" he asked.

"Nothing," she said, adjusting her towel.

Jack reached out and gently took her hand. Within a second
she was down on the bed, beside him. He leaned over. "What
happened with Matt? What did he say?"

"It's not Matt," she said.

Jack sighed and stood. "Katie, I probably shouldn't have
told you how I feel like that. I just… Well, I wanted you to
know. It seemed silly to put off any longer saying the words
that should've been spoken years ago. But I don't have any
expectations. I certainly don't want you to feel pressured to
return my feelings."

Return his feelings? Did he not have any idea who she was?
Her life had always been defined by him. Matt was right, he
never had a chance. There was never a doubt as to who had
a claim on her affection. But Matt was also correct when he
said love wasn't enough. As Jack had admitted, he loved her
when he left before. He loved her now and he was leaving
again.

They had little time left together, just as she'd suspected.
But what about her business? Did he have enough time to
help her save it?

"Jack," she said, "you think your board will approve a
loan, don't you?"

Jack glanced away. "No," he said. "I never really did."

"What?"

"I knew it would be a tough sell. It has to be a personal
loan."

"No," Katie said. She sat up straight. "I can't accept you money."

"It's the only way to save your paper," Jack retorted.

"But I don't understand. You wanted me to meet you board...."

"I wanted you to inspire others to invest in Newport Falls You need more than a loan, Katie. This town needs business.'

For a moment she was quiet. Then she stood up and faced him, crossing her arms. "I can't take a million dollars from you."

"You're not. That's why it's called a loan. I'll get my money back. And then some."

"What if you don't?"

"I will," Jack said.

"What if something happens?"

"Well, then," Jack said. His hands slipped around her. A devilish smile crept up his lips. "We'll have to renegotiate."

His fingers swept under her towel, but Katie brushed him away.

"We made love, Katie. I can't forget that." He shrugged and said, "The rules have changed."

"I bet you say that to all the girls." Katie winced as the words came out of her mouth. She was acting like a jealous schoolgirl again instead of a mature woman who knew the rules.

"Is that what's bothering you?"

"You have a...certain reputation," she admitted. The Iceman. Love 'em and leave 'em.

Jack shook his head. "I didn't want that reputation, believe me. But as much as I may have tried, I could never fall in love with any of those women."

"Why?"

"Because they weren't you. And it didn't matter who shared my bed. You already had my heart, Katie. You still do."

Katie could feel her heart break. She couldn't do this. She

couldn't endure this charade any longer. How could he tease her, knowing that he was leaving? Or perhaps that was the only reason he felt safe sharing his feelings. He knew the Atlantic Ocean would soon interrupt their romance. She was in the same position as his other women, as much as he denied it.

"I have to get to work," Katie heard herself say. "Everyone is waiting for me."

"You've been gone for two days. What's one more?"

"I need to go."

"Fine," Jack said. He smoothed her damp hair away from her forehead. "Truth be told, I have some business to take care of myself."

Katie hesitated. "In the city?"

"Yes," Jack said. "Listen, Katie, if you prefer we stick to business, so be it. But I'll be back here waiting for you at the end of the day."

"I have plans."

"Cancel them," Jack said. "If you don't want to see me for pleasure, do it for the town you love so much. You and I need to find a place for Franklin to put his factory. In the meantime, get dressed," he said. "I'll drive you to work."

Jack left her room, shutting the door behind him. Katie dressed as quickly as she could. She tried to suppress her excitement at the knowledge that Jack would be coming back again that evening. What did it matter? It was only going to make her pain worse in the end.

They drove to the paper in silence. When they arrived at her building, Jack said, "I'll pick you up at six."

He leaned over and gave her a kiss she swore she would remember the rest of her life. When Katie got out of his car, at least ten sets of eyes were focused on her. All were people who worked for her. As Jack sped away, she said good morning and walked up the steps with as much dignity as she could manage. She didn't even attempt an explanation. She was aware that every single one of her employees knew she had spent the last two days with Jack.

They all feigned nonchalance, which only confirmed that as far as they were concerned, the gossip was true: Katie Devonworth had been playing with fire.

And it *was* true, she reminded herself. She could feel herself getting sucked into the flames.

Katie pushed open the heavy door and escaped into the dimly lit building. As she looked around the old, stately hall she felt an immediate sense of relief. She was surrounded by family history. Her father and grandfather had both spent almost their entire lives in this building. They had both been motivated by a keen sense of responsibility to the paper and to the people they employed. It was a responsibility that had been passed on to Katie. As she climbed the stone steps to her office on the second floor, she could feel herself gaining strength with every step. This was her territory. She was safe here. Despite the problems and the pressure of financial hardship, she knew what to expect. She could handle it.

She walked into her office. She hung up her coat and sat behind the big oak desk. The desk was old, almost an antique, and the wear was apparent. It had been in this same office for almost fifty years. Her grandfather had purchased it when he started the paper and it had been there for her father when he took her grandfather's place. It had been waiting for her the day her father died and left the paper to her, his only child.

Katie turned on her computer and went online.

Jack was featured on page six of the *Wall Street Journal*, just as Matt had said. There was a picture of him beside a short story about his company's expansion into Europe. "This," Jack was quoted as saying, "is the chance of a lifetime. The fulfillment of a dream."

Katie leaned back in her chair. She closed her eyes, reeling from the impact of Jack's quote. *The fulfillment of a dream. The chance of a lifetime.*

He was leaving in less than two weeks.

The writing was on the wall. As much as she wanted to believe otherwise, her instinct was correct. Regardless of what Jack said, the end result would be the same. No matter how he felt, or thought he felt, she would get burned.

His actions made his tenderly spoken words meaningless. And she shouldn't have needed the article for proof. After all, if he had always loved her, why hadn't he told her?

"Hey," Marcella said. "You're back."

Katie glanced up at her old friend. "How are you?"

"The question is, how are you? You look terrible," Marcella said. "What happened? Did the financing fall through?"

"No," Katie said. "We're getting our money."

"So what's wrong? Did Bell Computers reject us?"

"No. There's nothing definite, but as far as I know, they're still interested."

"It's Matt, isn't it? My mom told me she saw him in town. That snake. Is he bothering you?"

"I saw him, but it's not Matt."

Marcella smacked her head. "Because it's Jack. Of course."

Katie sighed. "He says he loves me."

Marcella was silent for a moment. Finally, she shrugged. "Okay. The man you've loved your whole life tells you he loves you. Where's the sad part?"

Katie swung her computer screen around so that Marcella could read the page. When she was finished, Marcella said, "What did Jack say about this?"

"He hasn't even mentioned it to me."

"Talk to him, Katie. Maybe the article is wrong. Maybe he's not moving after all."

"No," Katie said. "I know it's the truth. I can feel it."

"Maybe he's just waiting for the right time to tell you."

"When might that be?"

"Maybe he wants you to go with him."

Katie shook her head. "Jack knows I could never leave Newport Falls. I could never leave the paper."

"Why not?" Marcella asked. She walked around and sat on Katie's desk. "I know your parents wouldn't want this paper to be your whole life. They would want more for you."

"Not that he's asked me, mind you, but even if he did, I couldn't. This is my home. I belong here."

"Let's face it," Marcella said. "Without Jack's money and connections, none of us will have a home here much longer."

Katie somehow made it through the day. At about four thirty Jack's assistant called. Snow was falling in New York and Jack's departure had been delayed. Katie could either go home or stay at work. Jack would find her.

Katie was not surprised that Jack had flown back to New York. He wouldn't know what to do with himself in a small town all day. And she doubted his work would be able to survive without him. Jack wouldn't hesitate at the expense of flying back and forth on a whim.

She wondered what it would be like to use a plane like some people use a taxi. For a moment she fantasized about Jack living in Newport Falls and commuting to work in the city. She shook her head. She couldn't seem to help herself from fantasizing about a future together, no matter how hard she tried.

When she finally left the building, getting a ride home from a co-worker, a light snow was falling. She stepped outside, pausing to button her coat. She adjusted her scarf and looked up, expecting to see Marcella, her ride home. Jack was standing at the foot of the steps, waiting for her.

"Hi." He smiled.

Katie could feel her heart melt at the sight of him. He was dressed for work. His black hair, naturally tousled that morning, was slicked back. The jeans jacket was gone. In its place was a cashmere coat and leather gloves. All together, the effect was intoxicating. He was the most handsome man she had ever laid eyes on.

"Hi," she managed to say.

He held out his hand. Katie walked down the steps, as if descending a promenade. She waved off Marcella down the street and took Jack's hand as he escorted her into the same car in which he had driven her to work that morning.

When he got inside, he said, "I was thinking we could take look at—"

"The old Hossmer warehouse?"

Jack smiled and nodded. "Exactly."

At one point in time Hossmer's had been the largest manufacturer of patio equipment in the United States. In the 1970s they had made millions manufacturing wrought-iron patio sets, which were sent around the world. When old Mr. Hossmer died in 1977, the business was inherited by his son. Within ten years, he had declared bankruptcy. Since then the building had lain dormant.

It was huge, at least eighty thousand square feet of unused, clean space. But the roof was falling down and the plumbing was in dire need of an update.

Still, anyone familiar with the building knew it had potential. And Jack knew it well. She, Matt and Jack had spent several high-school evenings wandering around the deserted halls. She knew that Jack had even spent the night several times after fights with his father.

Jack turned his car around. He started his windshield wipers. "How was your day?" he asked.

There was something sweet about their interaction that stirred Katie's heart. It was as if they were an old married couple. As if her husband had dropped her off at work and was now picking her up. As they drove down Main Street, she remembered how she and her mother would sometimes go to the office to pick up her father. They would wait at the foot of the steps for him to arrive, just as Jack had waited for her. She remembered the way her mother's face had lit up every time she saw the man she had spent a lifetime loving. Katie could still picture her parents walking down Main Street, arm in arm, side by side.

Once again, Katie forced herself to remember the artic
about Jack moving. She couldn't allow herself to be lull
into complacency by an artificial sense of domestic bliss. Sh
had to keep her distance. No matter how much she care
about Jack, they would never enjoy such a domestic scen
"My day was fine," she said.

Jack reached for her hand. He brought it to his lips an
kissed it. "Good," he said.

Katie could feel her resolve fade. "It's up here on th
right," she said.

"I remember," Jack replied.

The giant building looked as if it had been dropped int
the middle of the tundra. At least five feet of snow surrounde
it. Neither driveway nor parking lot had been plowed.

Jack parked on the road. So anxious was she to get awa
from Jack that as soon as he stopped the car, Katie opene
the door.

"Can you make it out?" Jack asked, nodding toward th
drift of snow beside her.

"Sure," she said. She took a step and sunk down. Jac
grabbed her hand and pulled her out. Together, they trudge
their way to the front door. Jack yanked on it, but it didn
open.

"It's not locked, is it?" Katie asked.

"It's hard to tell," Jack said. "The snow is so deep." H
glanced around the facade of the building. It still had remnant
of its former glory. The grounds were still framed by larg
and stately oak trees. The building stood four stories, its mar
ble facade chipped and stained but still beautiful. The elabo
rate stone eagles on top still hovered above their perch.

Jack nodded toward a broken window on the second floo
"I can get in through there."

"It's too high," she said. But he didn't hear her. Jack ha
already jumped up on a tree and was in the process of swing
ing himself toward the window.

"Be careful," Katie called.

Katie was suddenly reminded of Jack climbing in the burning house to rescue puppies. Underneath his expensive clothes, he still had the same athletic muscular form of the teenager he once was.

She held her breath as Jack jumped inside the building. He leaned out, grinning from ear to ear. "I'll be right down," he said.

Minutes later, she heard a noise. Jack was five feet in front of her, opening a window on the first floor. "Climb in here," he said.

Katie didn't hesitate. She grabbed Jack's hand and he pulled her up. Katie fell inside, knocking Jack down as she landed on top of him.

His strong arms were wrapped protectively around her. It was so dark she could barely make out his face, although it was mere inches away.

Katie attempted to roll off Jack, but he held her tight. "Not so fast," he said.

"You'll get your coat dirty," she replied.

"So?"

Katie felt the bulge of the flashlight in his coat pocket. "Is that a flashlight, or are you just happy to see me?"

Before he could answer, she pulled the light out and rolled off him. She shined the beam around the room. It was cavernous, empty with the exception of an old metal desk in the corner.

There was something so inherently sad about it. Katie could remember visiting an aunt who had worked there back in the days when the building had teemed with life. She remembered her aunt's personal tour of the plant. In every room they were greeted cheerily by neighbors and friends.

Now all that was left of the main production room was a desk.

"Come on," Katie said, holding out her hand to Jack. He took it, but instead of letting go when he got up, he pulled her close.

"I know what you're thinking," he said quietly. "I was here in those days, too. Maybe we can bring it back to life."

At that moment, Katie forgot about Jack moving. It didn't matter how much he loved her or how little. What mattered was that she loved him. Regardless of what the future held, she was with him right then. And for that, she was grateful.

He nodded around the room. "I used to sleep here every now and then," Jack said. "I kept a sleeping bag rolled up under a desk."

The sleeping bag had been brown with green trim. Katie had seen it there, tucked discreetly away. Although Jack had been too proud to admit it back then, she knew this old warehouse had become his refuge from his drunken father. "I wish you would've stayed with us instead, Jack. You were always welcome."

"I couldn't," he said. "I didn't trust myself around you."

"You didn't?"

"You were all I thought about, Katie. Every time I closed my eyes I would see you. I could feel you. I could imagine what it might be like to make love to you."

"But you never said anything. I never knew."

"I didn't want us to end up like my parents." Katie knew the story. Although Jack never spoke of it, Matt had told her that Jack's unwed mother had died in childbirth. That her family had blamed his father and hadn't wanted anything to do with Jack, their only grandson. Jack said, "I would never allow that to happen to you."

He brushed the hair away from her eyes and kissed her softly on the lips. Katie looped her arms around his neck and pulled him to her, responding to his kiss. In between kisses he said, "I wanted to wait until we were ready." Suddenly he was walking her backward, to the desk.

The flashlight fell to the ground, coating the room in darkness. With his lips still on hers, he took off his coat and tossed it over the desk. After ungloving his hands, he pulled at the buttons on her coat, undoing them one by one. When he was finished, he opened it up and pulled out the turtleneck she had tucked neatly into her skirt.

It was cold in the warehouse, but she didn't feel chilled. As Jack's fingers touched her bare skin, she felt a surge of heat rip through her. The glimmer of the moon cast a hazy glow in the room, creating an almost otherworldly effect.

Jack pulled back and looked at her. They paused, eye-to-eye, both enjoying the teasing, pleasurable warmth that came with the promise of what was to come. Still maintaining eye contact, Jack slowly pushed up her bra.

He knelt before her and ran his tongue under and around her breasts, working his way up to her nipples. He tickled them with his tongue and took them in his mouth, all the while holding her shirt up with his hands. The feeling building inside her was so intense, she felt dizzy and weak.

Jack must have sensed this, because at that moment he leaned her back gently on the table, so that her bottom half was resting on the edge. He reached under her skirt and pulled her pantyhose down to her boots.

As she felt Jack's heated breath against her most private part, she grabbed the edge of the table with her hands. She held on for dear life, feeling the wicked pleasure as Jack licked and teased her. It was wild and uninhibited, pure and total lust. She forgot about where they were, but it wouldn't have mattered even if she hadn't. All she could think about was Jack's tongue and the feeling building inside her. Jack sucked and licked, expertly running his tongue up and around her thick, damp folds.

"Take me," she said. "Now."

He penetrated her, filling her with his engorged self. The pleasure of him rubbing inside her was so exquisite, she found herself arching her hips and thrusting herself toward him, pulling him deeper and deeper.

She let go of the desk and placed her hands on his head. She pulled him toward her, slipping her tongue in his mouth. The sound of him moaning with excitement was electrifying.

She ran her tongue around the inside of his mouth, searching and feeling, probing and exploring much like he had explored her. She wanted to stay like that forever, the two of them entwined together, connected like a puzzle that was meant to fit together. But she could only hold back the dam of sensual gratification for so long. When it finally began to break, both stopped moving as release rocked through them at the same time, searing them into each other.

Afterward, Katie smiled. She was certain anyone walking in on them would be shocked to see the town good girl half-naked in a frigid warehouse, a man inside her. And she couldn't blame them. It was shocking…but not surprising.

For, thanks to Jack, she was now a woman who was as hot and passionate as she was alive.

But her sexual enlightenment was temporary. She had no doubt that when Jack returned to Europe, the ice princess would freeze once again.

She held him against her, running her fingers through his hair. Jack lifted himself above her and tenderly kissed her forehead. He bent before her, gently pulling up her hose and adjusting her skirt. Katie watched him, enjoying the loving gesture. He continued dressing her, tenderly fixing her bra and tucking her shirt back into her skirt.

When he was done, Jack took her hand and pulled her to her feet. She reached around and took his coat off the desk. She knocked the dust off it and looped it over his shoulders. He caught her hand again and pulled her to him. "Katie," he began, "I want you to understand—"

She held a finger to his lips, quieting him. She knew from the tone of his voice he was about to say something serious, and she didn't want anything to break the lovely spell that hung in the air.

Jack smiled. She gave his hand a tug and together they explored the rest of the building, neither saying a word.

When they were finished, they walked back to the window. Jack crawled out. He held out his hand to Katie and assisted her out. Then he jumped back up and shut the window. When he was finished, he brushed the snow off his pants and said, "Thanks for the personal tour."

Katie smiled. "Which tour?"

"Both," Jack said. Arm in arm, they walked back to the car.

When they arrived back at Katie's house, Jack made a fire and they settled down together on the sofa, wrapped in a blanket. All in all, it had been a perfect ending to an eventful day. After rushing to find Katie this morning, he had returned to New York and informed his staff he would not be going to Europe. It had been an easy and simple decision, for he had little choice. He couldn't leave Katie, not now or ever. He'd been given a second chance and he was not going to allow her to slip past him again.

He needed to prove to her he would do whatever it took to win back her love. He was glad for that morning, glad to have finally dealt with Matt. If Katie hadn't been there, however, his interaction with his former friend would not have ended so civilly. But the truth of the matter was, Jack could no longer harbor anger toward Matt. Whatever his sins, he was being punished. He had lost Katie. And that, as Jack knew from personal experience, was the worst fate possible.

No, he didn't have to worry about Matt bothering Katie. And if he did, well, he would be here to protect her. For he was now the official owner of Berman's department store. And he himself would oversee the opening of their new store in Newport Falls. He would work to bring business back into the town, offering incentives just like he had offered Franklin Bell.

Jack had mentioned the Hossmer warehouse to Franklin that morning, but Franklin had balked. He claimed that he didn't want to spend the money needed to renovate a building from the early 1900s, a building that had been empty for years. So Jack had offered a solution. He would invest in

Franklin's company, giving him the money needed to renovate the building.

"I hope you know what you're doing," Carol had said
when he approved the deal.

But as risky as it seemed to his employees, Jack had no
qualms whatsoever. For once in his life the path he was taking
seemed sure.

He hadn't told Katie about any of this. Nor had he told her
he had just bought Berman's. He knew she would never have
allowed him to make that financial sacrifice. And he didn't
want her to feel obligated to him.

"What are you thinking about?" It was Katie stirring
alongside him and breaking into his thoughts.

"You," Jack said. "The future."

"Let's not think about that," Katie said. "Let's just enjoy
our time right now."

As Jack wrapped his arms around her slender shoulders and
felt her head rest gently on him, he knew he wouldn't be able
to wait much longer. He would soon give her the ring that
had always been meant for her.

And, for the second time that day, he whispered, "I love
you, Katie. I always have."

But Katie didn't answer. She was already fast asleep. He
rested his head against hers and closed his eyes. It didn't
matter if she didn't hear him. He had the rest of his life to
prove his love to her. And he would not waste a single minute.

Eleven

Katie glanced at the layout in front of her. She forced herself to focus, but it was difficult. Franklin Bell was in town inspecting the warehouse. The entire town had worked hard so that the long-abandoned building might look more attractive to a prospective buyer. The driveway and parking lot had been plowed. The warehouse's windows had been opened to air out the building, and the old floors had been washed and polished.

But Katie was still nervous. "It'll be okay," Jack had told her again this morning. "Don't worry." Jack had been wonderful. She didn't know what she would've done without him. He had worked tirelessly, doing everything from scrubbing floors to flying Franklin out in his private plane. If she hadn't known Jack was moving to London, she would've thought he had changed his mind about Newport Falls. She would've thought that perhaps he was beginning to like it here. And perhaps he was. But it didn't matter. For Jack was leaving in two days.

She still hadn't mentioned his departure. Neither had he. It was as if they both understood that their time together was precious yet limited. Still, several times Katie had found herself tempted to ask him to stay. But what purpose would it serve? She couldn't imagine living anywhere else, and Jack would never be happy living in Newport Falls. It would be like caging a tiger who belonged in the wild. Jack needed to be free, to roam the world as necessary. He did not need to be encumbered with wife and town.

Katie stood up, pausing at the window. She stared down at the familiar scene beneath her. Once again she saw her parents walking hand in hand down the street, nodding hello to friends and family.

Her parents' reality had become her fantasy. But that was all it would ever be. For as of tonight, her fantasy was over.

Jack was taking her out to dinner. He had told her there was something that they needed to discuss. Something that could not wait.

Katie could almost hear him now. He would tell her that although he loved her, he needed to go. And despite her promises to herself, she would be devastated.

But she could not let Jack see her cry. He had been so good to her, so kind. She didn't want him to feel guilty for leaving her once again.

"It's all coming together," Marcella said. She was standing in Katie's doorway. "It's official. Berman's is coming in."

For a moment, Katie forgot her sadness. Her knees buckled underneath her as her heart jumped. Berman's!

"Whooeeee!" Katie let out a holler she was certain could be heard by the entire town.

"And," Marcella added, laughing at Katie's reaction, "I've already got an appointment with the advertising director. They want to take out a contract for two pages a week!"

That would more than double their advertising revenue. Katie closed her eyes as relief flooded through her. Her paper—

the business that had been in her family for generations—was saved. And it was all due to Jack.

"You'll have to call Jack and tell him," Marcella said. "Things are looking up." She walked away, humming.

Katie opened her eyes and glanced out the window. Once again, she vowed that Jack would not see her cry. She owed him that much and more. Much more.

Jack checked his watch. He was running late. He had stopped at the bank in Albany to get the ring out of the security box. He could feel the ring burning a hole in his pocket as he drove. He wasn't sure he could wait until dinner to give it to her. But he had to. He wanted this night to be perfect.

He was taking Katie to her favorite restaurant, the old inn on Main Street. It was a perfect setting for romance, a restaurant lit only by candles with a large stone fireplace and the stately elegance of a bygone era.

Jack had booked the entire dining room, giving Mrs. Crutchfield enough money to close for a week if she desired.

As he pulled into Katie's driveway, his fingers tightened around the steering wheel in anticipation. He parked the car and bounded out. Katie opened the door as he leapt up the stairs. Her brown hair was swept up, and she was wearing a black flowered dress that seemed to cling to all the right places. "Hi," he said. Damn, he thought. She looked beautiful.

"You could've just beeped," she said, grabbing her coat. "I would've come out."

Her lips looked full and ripe, ready to kiss. He leaned forward and touched them with his own. Katie wrapped her arms around him and kissed him as if her life depended on it. "Wow," Jack said, when they finally broke for air. "What did I do to deserve this?"

"You're you," Katie said.

Katie had called him after she found out about Berman's. He'd gotten so much pleasure from hearing the tone of her voice, the excitement as she spoke. He was glad he hadn't told her earlier. He'd thought about it, but had decided it was better to have her find out through the normal channels. He didn't want her to know that he was the owner until he proposed. As much as he trusted in their love and future, he didn't want her to feel obligated in any way.

Katie flashed him a gentle smile, just enough to make his heart skip a beat.

She brushed past him, her clean, fresh scent lingering behind.

Jack closed her car door and walked around to his side.

"Where are we going?" she asked as he got in.

"I thought we'd go to the inn...if that's all right with you."

She was quiet. Then she said, "I don't know if she's still open. She closes early on weeknights."

"Mrs. Crutchfield's expecting us," he said.

Jack drove to the restaurant as Katie chatted about her day. Jack smiled as he took her hand. For the first time in his life, he felt content.

He parked the car on Main Street, directly outside the inn. He opened Katie's door and together they walked inside, arm in arm.

Mrs. Crutchfield met them at the door with her usual cheerful smile. She was in her early sixties, pleasantly plump with long white hair swept up in a tight bun on the top of her head. She kissed them both and welcomed them like long-lost friends. She winked at Jack as she led them into the dining room. Jack had requested that the tables be set as usual. He didn't want to make Katie suspicious.

"It's quiet," Katie said. "Slow night, huh?"

Mrs. Crutchfield looked at Jack and winked once again. "You could say so."

Jack pushed in Katie's chair and sat down. He picked up the menu in a halfhearted attempt to prevent Mrs. Crutchfield from winking again and blowing his surprise. "I'll let you take a look at the menu," Mrs. Crutchfield said as she turned to leave. She grabbed Jack's shoulder and gave it a friendly pinch, which he was certain was delivered with a wink, as well.

But if Katie had noticed, she didn't mention it. "The prime rib is really good" was all she said.

"I remember," Jack said. He put down his menu. "I think it's the best in the country."

"See?" Katie said, grinning. "Newport Falls does have the best something."

"Katie," Jack said, leaning forward. "I like Newport Falls. I really do."

"When you were younger, you didn't."

"Well, that was then. Sometimes you have to leave home to appreciate it."

Katie glanced away. "So," she said, "how's it going with Franklin?"

"Great," Jack said. He had given him a tour of the town before showing him Hossmer's. Although his friend would never admit it, Jack could tell he was impressed with not only the town, but the building, as well. He had been particularly impressed to learn that the townspeople had taken it upon themselves to clean it up, just so it might look more presentable.

"Where is he now?" Katie asked.

"Happily ensconced in his hotel room, where I left him."

Mrs. Crutchfield returned to the table. "Have you decided?" She took their orders, winked once again and left.

Jack did his best to make small talk for a while, but a change had come over Katie. She seemed distant and preoccupied. Something was wrong. Did she suspect his intentions? After all, the clues weren't exactly subtle: her favorite restaurant, an empty dining room, a winking proprietress.

"Is everything all right?" he asked.

"Of course," she said quickly.

Mrs. Crutchfield came back carrying two steaming platters of food. Jack could see her looking at Katie's ring finger, checking to see if it was still bare. He shook his head and she nodded at him.

"I'll leave you two alone now," she said, practically beaming.

When she was gone, Katie cut into her meat and took a small bite. "I'm so grateful to you, Jack. I appreciate your help more than you know."

"I'm happy I'm able," he said.

They ate their meals in silence. After a while, Jack put down his fork and touched her hand. Katie almost jumped.

He held her hand. "What's wrong?"

"Nothing," she replied. She smiled once more, as if to prove her well-being.

Jack hesitated. He thought back to her greeting. Would she have kissed him like that if she wasn't happy to see him? Perhaps he was imagining things because he was nervous. "Katie," he started, then cleared his throat. "I have something I want to say." He paused. This was the speech he had waited a lifetime to give. He was ready. "You're all I think about, Katie. All the time."

Katie squirmed in her seat, as if uncomfortable. Jack glanced down at the table and kept going. "For too long I blamed everyone but myself for the loss of you—Matt, you yourself, and even fate. But I realized the only person to blame was me. I should've told you how I felt about you long ago. But I didn't. And because of that, I hurt you. Not to mention what I did to myself."

Jack lifted his head. Katie was looking toward the door. He touched her chin and steered it back, so that she was looking at him.

"Katie," he whispered, "do you forgive me?"

"What are you talking about?" she asked, glancing away once again. "There's nothing to forgive. Nothing."

"I was an idiot. I just assumed everyone in Newport Falls knew, including you. I loved you, Katie."

"I felt the same way," she said softly.

"I was so afraid of losing you. Of turning into my father. No job, an alcoholic…the town bum."

"I never thought of your dad like that," she said. "He lost his mind and soul when your mother died. I always thought he was a tragic, romantic figure. Besides, I never saw you as a reflection of your father."

He reached inside his pocket and felt the small box.

"It was fear, Katie. Fear kept me from you."

But he could tell she was no longer listening. Instead she said, "I wanted to thank you for what you've done to help me. To help the town. I appreciate it more than you know."

He ignored her remark and continued with his well-rehearsed speech. "I have a lot of making up to do with you, Katie. I've already told you that I've often thought about that day at the creek and how different it would have been if I had told you how I felt."

"I know." Katie's eyes welled with tears. "And these last few weeks have been wonderful. But it's too late, isn't it? We've missed our chance."

Jack was stunned. "What?" he heard himself ask.

"I think we both know where this is going."

"Do we?"

"I know what you're about to say, Jack. And if you really do love me, please, don't say it. I can't bear it."

Jack felt as if she had kicked him in the stomach. She did not want to marry him. But she loved him, didn't she? She hadn't said as much, but he could feel it, feel it in the way she looked at him. In the way she made love to him. Was he mistaken? "Katie," he asked, "do you love me?"

"What does it matter?"

"It matters to me."

She shook her head. "Matt was right. Sometimes love isn't enough." She stood up.

Jack could feel his life slipping away. "Tell me what I need to do, Katie. Tell me what I can say."

"There's nothing left to say," she said, turning to leave.

Jack jumped up and grabbed her hand, stopping her.

"I can't do this anymore," she said, starting to cry. "I'm sorry, but I can't." She pulled away from him. "Please, Jack. If you love me, say goodbye."

And just like that, she was gone. Jack wanted to run after her and stop her, but to do so would be to go against her wishes. He suddenly realized what Katie had been trying to tell him all along. No wonder she hadn't wanted to speak of the future. Because the future, her future, did not include him.

He heard the words he knew would haunt him for the rest of his life. *If you love me, say goodbye.* He was too late. And he would forever pay the price.

Twelve

The mayor's office was in a plain brown brick building on Main Street. There were several other offices in the building, as well, including the town dentist and pediatrician. Normally, Katie enjoyed visiting there. All three men—the dentist, the pediatrician and the mayor—had been friends of her father's. She had known them her entire life and they all treated her like a favorite niece. Their meetings typically took on the boisterous air of a family reunion. But even the thought of seeing old friends didn't cheer Katie.

She checked her watch as she walked up the narrow flight of stairs, heading toward the meeting with Franklin Bell and the mayor. She wondered if Jack would be there, as planned, or if he had already left town.

She had lain awake all night, thinking about Jack. Did he really think she didn't know what he wanted to talk to her about? Did he think that she would be able to sit there and listen quietly? To stretch out an already painful goodbye?

Still, she missed him already. Her house seemed empty without him, her life and future barren.

But she would not let him know that. No. She owed it to Jack to keep it together. She knew it was a tall order. After all, she hadn't managed very well the previous evening. But today, today would be different. She had another chance at dignity. She didn't want his pity. Not now or ever.

As she turned the corner she froze. Jack's voice echoed through the hall. *He was there.*

But, of course. He was Jack Reilly, after all. And this was business.

Her heart in her throat, she stood at the end of the hall. The office door was open and she could see the three men sitting around a small, round table.

Mayor Herb Watkins waved. "Hello, Katie." He stood up and motioned for her to join them. "Come on in."

Franklin stood as she approached, and reluctantly, it looked, Jack followed suit. Jack gave her a quick glance and nod before sitting back down. He was in his work attire. His hair was slicked back and he was wearing one of his expensive suits with a silk tie.

Much to her horror, the mayor scooted his chair over and drew up another one, right next to Jack. She slid into the narrow space and sat down.

She was so close to Jack, her leg was brushing up against him. She could smell his cologne and almost taste his minty breath. It was all she could do to focus.

"Like I was saying," Franklin said, "my factory would employ three hundred people. Even if we have a building that we can use as a factory, we'll need more than that to convince these people to move here."

Jack spoke up. "Franklin, this town is Americana at its best. It's the closest to Mayberry you'll find anywhere. I think that's what people are looking for nowadays, don't you? A beautiful place with clean air and safe streets."

Jack's hand brushed hers. She inhaled sharply as a current

of sexual energy ran through her. But the touch was clearly an accident. Jack shifted in his chair, moving away from her.

"And I heard," the mayor said, looking at Franklin, "that another department store may be moving into Holland's." Herb was known to get carried away at times and say things that, although not outright lies, were more half-truths. "I'm a politician" was what he said in his defense. And everyone agreed that it was as good an excuse as any. But this time he spoke the truth.

Katie told the mayor so. "I thought you knew. Berman's department store is moving in."

Franklin turned toward Jack and asked, "Is the deal final?"

Jack nodded. "Yes."

"So you own a department store now." He chuckled.

Katie felt as if the world had come to a screeching stop. *What?* "You bought Berman's?" she asked Jack.

Jack glanced at her and then shifted his eyes away.

"He's put together quite a deal here," Franklin said.

"You..." Katie began weakly, still staring at Jack.

"*You're* going to open the store?" the mayor asked.

Franklin tried to set the record straight. "Jack is going to be in London, shopping at Harrods."

"I didn't know you were moving to London," the mayor said, looking confused.

When Jack sat in silence, Franklin looked up from his papers and asked Jack, "You *are* moving, aren't you?"

Jack glanced back at Katie. He paused as if waiting for her to speak. But what did he want her to say? And why hadn't he told her about Berman's? After a moment he said, "I guess there's no reason not to."

"And apparently, we're moving, too," Franklin said, closing his file of papers. "I'm in. We'll take over the Hossmer plant."

It was as if the room had started to spin. Katie saw the Hossmer warehouse sparkling like new, once again filled with people. She imagined the For Sale signs disappearing, long-closed stores reopening. It was as if she could see Newport Falls being reborn before her eyes.

"It seems like we have a lot to celebrate," the mayor said.

Franklin smiled. "I agree."

She turned toward Jack, possessed by the urge to throw her arms around him. He had done it. He had single-handedly saved Newport Falls.

"Thank you, Franklin," Jack said. "And congratulations. I know you won't regret it." He stood up. "I wish I could stay and celebrate, but I have to get back to New York."

Katie could feel her heart drop as her excitement disappeared. Jack was leaving. Would she ever see him again?

"Thanks for everything," Franklin said. The two men shook hands. "I can see why you're so fond of this place."

Jack shook hands with the mayor. When he was finished, he turned toward Katie. He didn't attempt to shake her hand. "Goodbye, Katie," he said with a curt nod.

"Thank you," she murmured.

And with that, he left the room.

Katie sat there, dumbstruck. Jack had bought Berman's.

He had saved the town with a million dollars from his personal account.

I love you, he had said. *I've always loved you.*

And suddenly the facts that just a few moments ago seemed to suggest a life without Jack, broke apart and came back together in a totally different way.

Jack had left Newport Falls not because he didn't love her, but because he did. He was afraid if they became involved romantically before they were ready, it would herald disaster. So he'd waited, working to guarantee them both a better life. And what did she do? She had repaid his devotion by marrying his best friend. It was she who had given up on them years ago, not him.

And she was about to make the same mistake again.

Suddenly, it didn't matter if she stayed in Newport Falls or not. This would no longer be home unless she was sharing it with Jack. One moment with him was worth a lifetime of pain without him. She had to follow her heart. And for once, her mind was in complete agreement. She needed to be with Jack, whatever the price. "I, uh, I'll be right back," she muttered. Without bothering to retrieve her coat, she left the meeting, chasing after the man she loved. The man she had always loved.

Clad in a turtleneck and wool skirt, she dashed outside, not even noticing the cold. She spotted Jack halfway down the street.

She took off running, slid on the ice and righted herself, cursing her impractical pumps. "Jack!"

Jack turned. He appeared startled to see her making her way toward him. "Take me with you," she yelled.

Once again she slipped on the ice, this time sliding into his arms. He dropped his briefcase and caught her before she fell.

"What?" he asked, holding her up.

A strong gust of wind blew a cloud of snow at her cotton shirt. "I love you. I've always loved you. And I want to be with you," she said. "I don't care if I have to move to do it."

"What are you talking about?"

"Take me with you to London."

"London?" he repeated. He looked at her curiously. Then he shook his head and said solemnly, "I can't."

She was too late. He had changed his mind. "But why?" she asked.

Jack smiled and said, "Because I'm not going to London."

It took a moment for the words to sink in. "But the article said you were moving tomorrow. That it was the chance of a lifetime...."

"Article?" he asked. "The one in the *Wall Street Journal*?"

She nodded.

"That article was written one week before you came back into my life. They just waited to run it."

So surprised was Katie, she could not speak.

"Is that what last night was about?" he asked. "Did you think I was going to leave you?"

Katie took a step backward and averted her eyes.

"Where's your coat?" Jack asked, unbuttoning his own.

"I was in a hurry," she said.

"How could you think I would move without saying a word?" He opened up his coat and pulled her in to him, wrapping the coat around them both. "Why didn't you talk to me about this?"

"I thought it was inevitable," Katie said. "I mean, you said you always loved me, but you left before. Why should this time be any different?"

"Everything is different," Jack said. "We're not kids anymore." He sighed and said, "But we still have some tough decisions."

"I'll move to the city," Katie said quickly. "I want to, really I do."

"Katie," Jack said. He cupped her chin and raised her face toward his. "I don't want you to leave Newport Falls."

Katie could almost feel her heart shatter. "Why not?"

"Because we both know you could never live anyplace else."

"But I want to be with you. I need to be with you."

Jack stood still. "I can feel your heart," he said. "I can feel it beating."

She slid her hands around and up his well-muscled belly. She put her palm against his chest so that she could feel the steady beat of his heart. "And I feel yours," she whispered.

"It's your heart, Katie. It belongs to you. It always has."

She glanced up at him and smiled. "So I can go back to New York with you?"

He shook his head. "No."

Her smile faded. "Why not?"

"Because I have a better idea."

"You do?"

"Maybe I should move here."

Katie wasn't sure she heard him correctly. She could've sworn Jack was talking about moving to Newport Falls.

"I have something for you," Jack said. "Reach into my pocket."

Katie did, and pulled out a small, red box.

"What is this?"

"This is what I wanted to talk to you about last night," he said.

She was trembling as she opened the lid to reveal a heart-shaped diamond ring with a ruby on either side.

"It was my grandmother's," he said. "I've been holding on to it all this time. I've wanted to give it to you for as long as I can remember."

He took off his coat and looped it over her shoulders. Then, right there in the middle of Main Street, he got down on one knee. "Katie Devonworth," he said, slipping the ring on her finger, "will you marry me?"

Katie looked at the ring. She had dreamed of this moment many times, but never had she imagined the feeling that spread through her, warming her heart. "Yes," she heard herself say.

He stood and kissed her. She could feel herself melt into him, accepting his love without reservation. Their bodies, like their hearts, were meant to be together.

"Come on," he said hoarsely. "Let's go home."

"Home?"

"I think we can both fit into that big old house of yours, don't you?"

Katie smiled as she adjusted the coat, wrapping it around both of them. Together they walked down Main Street, side by side, arm in arm.

And so, Katie Devonworth finally learned how to play with fire.

* * * * *

From *USA TODAY* bestselling author

Cait London

HOLD ME TIGHT

(Silhouette Desire #1589)

Jessica Sterling is concerned about a threat
to her best friend and is determined to secure
the best man for the job—unnervingly attractive
Alexi Stepanov. But Alexi is in no mood to take
orders from this sweet-talking siren, and decides
to make a few demands of his own....

HEART BREAKERS

*Available June 2004
at your favorite retail outlet.*

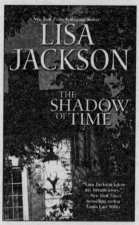

Award-winning author

Jennifer Greene

**invites readers to indulge in
the next compelling installment of**

The Scent of Lavender

The Campbell sisters awaken to passion
when love blooms where they least expect it!

WILD IN THE MOONLIGHT

(Silhouette Desire #1588)

When sexy Cameron Lachlan walked onto
Violet Campbell's lavender farm, he seduced
the cautious beauty in the blink of an eye.
Their passion burned hot and fast, but
could they form a relationship beyond
the bedroom door?

*Available June 2004
at your favorite retail outlet.*

COMING NEXT MONTH